As the Daisies Bloom

~ A Novel ~

Ethel brought them menus and small glasses of water. She and Maggie never worried whose table was whose. They helped each other in equal measure, and as far as anyone knew split everything left for them 50/50, though Maggie told me once it was 40/40/20 on weekends when a part-time dishwasher came into work. The dishwashers would never stay long. Regardless, Maggie and Ethel always gave a piece of their tips to whoever was washing dishes, pots and pans. They did their own table bussing, but they also both had started as dishwashers in other larger restaurants and had vivid memories of waitstaff and temperamental cooks who would loudly dump everything in the dish pans or sink and walk off as though their superior jobs didn't need to acknowledge the hard worker in the waterproof apron making everything sparkle for the next guests.

The dad offered a quiet, "Thanks."

"Coffee?"

"Sure—just black."

"Some kind of juice for the boys?" Ethel asked.

The father asked, "Boys, you want some orange juice?"

The younger boy nodded in the affirmative and the other gave a negatory head shake on juice. "I'd like a Coke." Was dad going to intervene on such a choice for breakfast? He just smiled and said, "Maybe you want a hot-fudge sundae to go with that and an order of fries?"

Ethel having heard no contradiction to the request was off to get the coffee, juice and Coke. The three quietly went about studying the menu, not that it takes much study. The Daisy Cafe, if they have a motto, would be stick to the basics. Maggie arrived with my bacon and three over-easy eggs, no toast, no potatoes—as per my routine—in one hand and the coffee pot in the other. She sat down the plate, filled my cup and asked the two boys, "What are your names?"

The older boy answered for both and added more information than requested. "He's Jimmy. I'm Johnny and our dad is Tyler. We're from Macon, Georgia."

Some instinct told the always out-going Maggie not to ask about their mother. She thought if Johnny wanted to shed light on

4

her name and whereabouts he would have. She left well enough alone for the time being.

Maggie waved off Ethel letting her know she'd get their order while she was there. Would Johnny go for that hot-fudge sundae? He ordered first.

"He pointed at my plate and said, "That's what I want.""

"Just like that?" Maggie asked.

"Yup, just like that."

His father corrected him, "Yes, ma'am, like the kind gentleman is having."

Maggie chuckled and said, "'Yup' works pretty well here. In fact better than 'yes, ma'am' but we'll respond to either. We don't get many gentlemen in here."

"What can I get you, Jimmy?"

Maggie and I both thought the dad might jump in for him, but he didn't. Jimmy got a big grin and said gigglingly, "Hot-fudge sundae sounds real good." Amused by himself for what he knew was going to be shot down by his dad, he was quick to add, "Scrambled eggs and white toast." Tyler ordered a mushroom Swiss omelette and a side of sausage. Hah—my Friday morning regular order. Noel, the cook, makes the best mushroom Swiss omelette I've had anywhere. Tyler made a good choice.

As I enjoyed my breakfast, the boys and their dad sat quietly. I was waiting for the smart phones to come out of their pockets, but they never did. I thought they perhaps were on extra good behavior since they had joined someone else's table, but it was plain enough, good behavior came pretty natural to these three. If I didn't know better I'd think they were Amish.

I looked at Johnny and said, "I've only been to Macon one time. I was in a choir in college and we sang at one of the churches there one Sunday. They had a big potluck lunch afterwards. It was the best food of our whole tour."

"What church was that?" Johnny wanted to know.

"Church of God."

Jimmy piped up, "That's our church!"

Tyler showed an interest in this revelation as well. He began to put two and two together as to how this old white man came to

5

sing in an all black congregation. "Did you go to Anderson College?"

"I did, though they 'upgraded' to Anderson University soon after I graduated. And if I'm honest, that was the first time I'd ever been in an all African-American church."

Tyler interjected, "You can say black church. That's what we are, though since you've been there we've changed some. A little more mix of the rainbow than in the old days. I'll bet it looked a little rough around the edges compared to those big Church of God churches in Anderson."

"It was a little culture shock for me. I grew up in a small farming community of mostly Mennonites, but I will say the welcome we got was Christianity at its best." I thought about adding that such was not saying much given the bigotry of so much of Christian America, but for the sake of the young boys, I held my tongue.

Tyler said it for me. "Christianity at its best can be hard to come by." I could sense Tyler might well have said more on the subject given more familiar surroundings and if the boys weren't in earshot.

Johnny looked a little bit surprised to hear his dad say what he did say, but Ethel had set the plates down quietly in the conversation and Johnny's momentary pause of curiosity was quickly reset for crunching on a piece of bacon. Maggie, assuming I was not going to leave them mid-meal, filled my coffee and refreshed all three drinks of my breakfast companions. As discreetly as possible I circled my index finger towards Maggie to give her the sign that I'd pick up their tab. She just as discreetly nodded in acknowledgement. I hoped my gesture wouldn't cause offense, but the few times I've done this for one reason or another in the past has always worked out okay. I didn't see any reason this wouldn't. I could always make the excuse of returning the generosity of the Macon church so long ago at that potluck lunch with ravenous college students.

It seemed to suddenly occur to Jimmy, "I bet Momma was at church that Sunday when the man sang there."

Johnny giggled. "He'd remember her!" Then looking at me with a smile from ear to ear he said, "She was the biggest person in that church. Bigger than any man!"

Tyler added, "No point in pretending the boy exaggerates. And she was faithful every Sunday and chief planner of every church meal. She was there, and so was I though I was too young to have much memory of the choir visit. Since you mentioned it, I do have some memory of it."

I didn't know for sure whether my confession was appropriate or not. The truth is I have very vivid memories of that church sanctuary, that spread of food and most vivid of all the biggest breasted woman I ever saw—before or since. It had to be their grandmother by their own account of her. She was tall and big all the way up and down, but featuring one part above all others it must be said, she was top heavy. I'd known a lot of strong Mennonite farm women with big families and accompanying big breasts but nothing in comparison to this Macon Georgia matriarch. I'd begun to think the restaurant was crowded that morning for the sole purpose of putting this young family at my table. Why, I still wasn't sure, but the worlds between us were shrinking quickly.

Jimmy spoke up, "Momma always said, 'I can't find a brazeer to fit me!' I asked daddy what a brazeer was, and he said its grandma's underwear tops."

It was time to fess up. "Well I can't say for certain, but by your description and her role in the food organizing, I have to say I remember your grandmother quite well. How is she?"

Johnny answered, "That'n dead."

"She died on my seventh birthday," Jimmy added.

Tyler sighed, "Ah, that was a good woman. She loved her babies. And Lord knows we all loved her. She needed a body that size to carry that heart of hers. It wouldn't have ever fit in anyone smaller. I always was afraid her size would kill her, but it never did. She was as big the day she died as she was when you saw her all those years ago. She was 83 when she passed just last year, and it took eight of us and a mighty big casket to take her to her resting place. She died at home in an oversized rocking chair that my Uncle Ira built for her. He is a real craftsman when it comes to anything with wood. The three of us spent much of our young lives

7

being rocked in that chair, nestled in those breasts of that dear woman. She told Ira about a year before her death that she wasn't likely to last too much longer. She'd found lumps in her breast but asserted she wasn't about to start letting doctors take over her life. I'm sure she was in pain—had to be, but she managed somehow to move between her bed which we had moved into the living room, the bathroom and that chair."

Johnny filled in some more details. "Momma always said when she pass that she wanted a big shrimp and crab boil at the church. She loved pickin' crab and if we ate around the edges she be standing over ya sayin', 'That ain't no way to eat crab, boy. Some Cajun gonna come along and snatch up what you're throwing out and show you how it's done.' So we had that boil and you couldn't have found enough to make one crab cake from what was thrown out."

"The boy sure is right about that." You could see the delight in Tyler's face that his boys should remember the grandma's instructions with such affection.

Tyler clarified the record a bit. "She was actually my grandmother but she raised me and I always called her Momma. I didn't call my grandfather daddy. He was some combination of both. I just called him Pappy."

I wrapped it up by looking at Tyler and saying, "So that was your momma. Well, you may not have her big frame, but as best I can tell you got that heart and so have these boys of yours. It has truly been a pleasure sharing this table with you. Truth is, I don't come in here on weekends because the parents and kids are on their cell phones with the little ones running around out of control. During the week we don't see many kids in here. If they were all like yours...."

Oh, I know most would have told that dad how proud he should be of those boys. That's not my way. I've no business apportioning out pride or shame. Mennonite roots—never could see how pride had become a virtue. I know shaming hasn't helped the world or the pride that keeps the honor and shame system going. I'd said all I needed to say. Part of the point of appreciating silence is to know when enough is enough. One look made it clear

I'd said enough. All three were in a place of what can only be called the joy of the moment as they remembered the old woman.

We were all done eating and both men coffee'd out. Maggie had picked up my debit card a minute or two earlier and was back with the receipt. Tyler asked for his and Maggie said, "Talk to the old man."

I just said, "Your momma fed me a feast. The least I can do is buy y'all's breakfast. It's been a real pleasure. I never thought I'd meet anyone from that Macon church ever again in my life." Expressing my curiosity from the get-go I asked, "What brings you to our town? Just passin' through?"

"We might be a permanent fixture. Remains to be seen. I'm here for an interview. The boys came along..." Tyler hesitated. "Well, why the boys are along is a long story." Taking each hand, rubbing the head of the boy to each side of him, he just smiled and finished, "but we'll not get into that now. It's about time for me to get where I need to go. We do thank you for breakfast and for the company."

In unison, without any prompting from their dad, both boys said, "Yes, thank you sir."

It occurred to me, thanks to Maggie, I knew their names but they didn't know mine. I said, "Johnny, you've gotten mighty formal from 'Yup' to 'Thank you, sir.' My name is August. Just like the month. If you boys move here and see me in the street or here in the Daisy Cafe, just say, 'Hey August.' And I'll say, 'Hey yourself.' We'll keep things informal if your dad's okay with that."

"I'm good with that," Tyler said. And with that they were on their way to wherever fate was to take them, or maybe better put to where that old black woman with a heart as big as her chest was workin' for them as she'd seemed to work out our chance meeting at the Daisy Cafe.

Just as Tyler was about to go out the door and I close behind, I asked him, "What was your momma's name?"

He turned his head with a big smile. "Margarette, but she insisted everyone call her Daisy. She loved daisies."

If he'd looked at me even a second longer, he'd've seen an old man's tears.

9

Chapter Two

I sauntered my way home running through a lot of old college memories—not just of that Macon Sunday morning, but certainly that one stuck central in my thoughts. When I got to the door of my apartment, ole Penny-girl was wound up as though I'd gone to Switzerland for a month leaving her home alone. I got her leash and said, "All right I'm a little past my time, but I haven't been gone that long!" I have gone to Switzerland on trips, though never for a month, and so I do know how she looks when I return. She likes to turn on the same drama for any excursion that goes longer than she deems necessary. When I stick to a predictable return time she's as likely to be napping in the closet as she is to be awake to greet me. I assured her I wouldn't make a habit of such extended breakfast outings.

As the two of us strolled through the yard I got to wondering. Did anyone else in the choir remember this woman who I now know to be Daisy? I'd guess most probably not. Possibly no one else. Did I remember it for some future encounter with her descendants at the Daisy Cafe? One does have to wonder about such improbable encounters.

Over the years, I've had my share of one-off experiences with people to appreciate the moments given to us that might well be remembered and not just remembered but consequential to someone's life. I can name my own with a dean of the college who saved me from despair without perhaps ever knowing just how much of a difference his kindness meant to me. Long after his death, I can single out that time when I made a course change in my life and how grateful I am for it. And I'm pretty sure of a few encounters where I was able to pay that attention and kindness forward, but it is as likely as not that we ever know the difference we made in that singular moment in someone's life.

I wondered if I would ever see Tyler and Johnny and Jimmy again. Would a small boy's voice turn my head in the street at him calling out, "Hey, August!" If he did, would my fellow citizens judge this young black boy for calling out so informally to an old white man? I hate to have those kind of thoughts, but let's keep it real. I know more than one of the ol' boys' table looked my way with the contempt they pretend to cover-up these days when those three sat down with me. They've proven themselves enough times for me not to be surprised or to hope for better from them. I always hope the non-whites who wander in don't pick up on it. Intuition of bigotry being what it is, I suspect they spot it in an instant.

I got my own odd looks over the years. I was well respected in the community by most, but there was a silent, disapproving undercurrent from a few. I'd lived with the same man, Miles, for thirty-five years. We both worked at the university and while we weren't active organizers for "identity" political causes or for same-gender marriage, when the law allowed, we went to a Boston courthouse. Even though the only thing that changed was the sheet of paper from the government, all plausible deniability was gone. Enough knew we'd gotten married to either congratulate us with great enthusiasm or to distance themselves as never before. One could never be sure which it was going to be. That the people we instinctively cared most about were congratulatory was a great relief. For a few, distancing wasn't quite enough. We were long time, faithful members of a church, and we suddenly found the boisterous few condemning us in new and mean-spirited ways. All efforts to reaching out were slapped away in an instant. After a few months of trying and failing we finally gave way. If that's the Christianity that defines them, then it is theirs to have with all the exclusion they love so dear.

When my spouse had the earlier-than-anticipated but fortunate death I wish for myself—dying quickly and peacefully—I honored what I knew he wanted. No service, cremation, ashes buried in our dog cemetery. We'd had our share of canine companions over those thirty-five years. Penny-girl's sister was the most recent departure.

A few from the church reached out when Miles died, and I came close to giving it one last try. Our experience had left its own mark on each of our friends at church too; I could see how much they had distanced themselves from church life while still attending more than not. So, maybe someday I'll go back. Not today.

Before our marriage, it seemed like there wasn't anything the church shied away from asking us to do. We both had a few basic

11

gifts any smaller church is eager to have. We could carry a tune, balance accounts, read a profit and loss statement, organize an annual stewardship drive, cook for a crowd, clean, paint and mow lawn. Who doesn't want all that? On top of our basic skill set they didn't mind the generous check in the plate once a month either.

Marriage was that step too far. If they had to bless us, they would have to be open to the notion of blessing others. Here we were causing the ever-splitting congregations to consider doing so again. I wrote as healing a letter as I could muster expressing my concern not for Miles and me, who were secure enough in our own skin after all these years, but for the young people who would have to face a church still judging them from the same cherry-picked verses used to condemn. Must we drive another generation of these young people and their friends from the church? So it would seem. Most depressing of all was the fact that the most vocal attack against us came from someone who was the primary leader of Christian education for the children and youth of the church. Apparently, her scripture cherry-picking had no trouble overlooking Timothy. She was anything but silent. I never liked the legalism for church management as laid out in Timothy, but she caused me to reconsider.

Less immediate but no less hard to take was the divide raging among the bishops and clergy of the larger church. When I sent a very private email to our own bishop, I soon found it disseminated to the various committees of the diocese. Without a response to me, he simply forwarded my email and copied me. He added nothing in his forward to them as to why my email was going to them. I was shocked and a bit horrified to be honest. He would apologize when I saw him next though he never explained why he felt compelled to breech my request for confidentiality. When he retired, the next one caused us a different kind of angst when his words never seemed to match his actions. He certainly loved the office and the trappings that went with it. All his vestments came from Rome. Once when he was processing in with cope, miter and crozier, I leaned over to Miles and said over the hymn we were singing, "Walk softly and carry a big stick." In fairness there was one truly stand-out retired bishop from England who filled in one holy week when we were without a priest. He was a truly humble man.   Certainly, that Easter every person knew they were welcomed.   Perhaps there is something in a name.   The gentle bishop's name was Lamb.   He seemed to me a true shepherd of the flock given to his watch.   But enough about bishops.

The hard shells didn't crack.   That fellow-church woman, who was our fieriest critic, finally said to a friend of ours, "They don't love Jesus."   News to us.   It was time to go.   Let the dead bury the dead.   Maybe not our best sentiment given our long history together, but if felt like an honest one at the time.

I suppose it seemed extra hard to comprehend because prior to the issuance of a marriage license, there had been times when the congregation seemed all in on our relationship—going so far as to want to have Miles ordained.   He was a gifted man when it came to teaching how to read the Bible and could breathe life into almost any old dusty character pulled from the good book.   I would consider myself his student in this regard.   He was a far better listener than me and most others.   And he could weep with the grieving with a sincere grief of his own.   I, on the other hand, am more the nuts and bolts practitioner who is better suited to getting the meal around after a funeral than consoling others.   His family were all huggers and my Swiss roots were far more reserved.   One hundred fifty years in this country hadn't changed the fact that for us—why hug when a handshake will do?   I'm quite willing to take it even one step further and get rid of handshakes.   Why shake hands when a simple reverent nod of the head will do?   Miles's Cajun roots were far more emotional and personal.   Since over time he'd learned to temper his anger, it was hard for those who knew him not to be drawn to the inherent support mechanism that was his personality. One obstacle or another always uprooted any hopes some of the church members had for his vocation as their pastor.   That's a long story, perhaps for another time.   I suspect if hierarchy and circumstance hadn't derailed the call to a pastoral vocation, the hidden resistance that surfaced after our marriage would have come to light in the "discernment" process, with the end result the same.

Penny-girl was in no hurry to go in.   As my mind wandered to these things, she pulled from spot to spot in the yard fixating every now and then on a particular one. Sniffing, sniffing, sniffing. These spots must be really good to a dog's nose. She was just enthralled with each one as though it was all new territory and new smells never before experienced. It certainly wasn't new territory, and whatever was drawing her to that spot was bound to have been a familiar smell after all these years. Oh, to have such enthusiasm at her age!

She was finally ready to go back in. She walked slowly behind me now. Ready to go in but not in any particular rush. When she and her sister were young I used to love to let them off the leash way down the drive, and they would haul-ass towards the door, dust and gravel flying as they went. Bonnie was about twice her size, but Penny-girl was all muscle and could out-run her without trying. As though to protect Bon's ego she would always slow down about twenty feet from the house so Bon' could proclaim victory. Bonnie would turn around as Penny approached the door, raising her front paws to slap Penny around a bit. Most of the time she'd ignore it, but every few times Penny-girl would bare her teeth as I approached, and they'd both be up on their back legs as though it was a fight to the death. It was all in fun. Not once did they draw blood. I loved to egg her on. "Uh, she mad now! Yea, she mad now. She's tearin' her up." They both seemed to like me cheering on the fight.

Her running days are over. Her fighting days long gone. At her age she's good for a pull to get to the first patch of grass for a pee and that's about it. We buried her sister more than a year ago. Penny-girl and I added Miles' ashes to the plot just a month later. Now it's just the two us and probably not two for much longer.

Back inside, my thoughts returned to the encounter with the boys this morning. I really was curious where Tyler was interviewing, but since he didn't offer any insight on that nor where the mother was and why the boys were in tow for the interview, I wanted to respect the limits between us more than I wanted my curiosity satisfied. If he had wanted to tell me more he would have.

Not so long ago, Penny-girl would have popped up on the back of the couch like a cat and looked out at the scenery while I settled in my leather swivel chair with my laptop to catch up on the all-depressing news around the world. These days, I was lucky if she stayed in the living room for a mid-morning nap let alone a dog's contemplation of the day as she looked out the windows. She was more likely to retire to her Orvis memory foam bed back in the bedroom where she could stretch out in comfort in the dim light and enjoy her dreams of chasing rabbits as she had done in her younger days. I could be sure she would reappear when I got around to making lunch. Her nose always could pick up on any raw meat coming out of the fridge. Until then, I was on my own in the front and she sound asleep in the back.

Before leaving for breakfast each morning I read a few regular things for basic inspiration. A poem, a meditation or two—varies a bit but something to set a course for gratitude for the new day. Once back home, I tackle the weightier matters of our world. I ease into it gradual like. First is news from a Swiss paper. They can seem to focus more on the good going on inside the country than the bad though they are pretty blunt about the bad when they see it needs to be called out. They even have occasional pieces on the richness of cultural traditions that I find particularly interesting. One of my favorites was a video piece on a family decking out their cows for the annual trek on their way to summer pastures. The entire town turns out to watch them as they go right through the village. It doesn't get much better than that for this old farm-boy.

Then I move on to news from the UK and finally ease into the depressing partisan parsing required to make any sense of what is going on in my own country. I'm not sure why that has to be such a challenge. When I was a boy we just turned on Walter Cronkite. I've learned enough about our history to know lies were covered up pretty well in those days. And that is not an endorsement for cover-up of lies. Those were certainly sins of deliberate omission. But it must be said that these days, blatant lies abound and that seems to be perfectly accepted. As long as your guy or gal is telling the lie you like to hear, then all is right with the world. It is no easy thing to realize that people you've considered friends for years seem to have lost their minds out of some blind devotion to the liar of choice. My mind went back to Tyler for a moment. Could that boy of Daisy's be one such shallow fellow? If I ever got to know him well, would a well-spring of disappointment come flowing out of some shallow shell of a man? I've seen such disappointments before. My egalitarian affections afforded him any benefit of doubt. I was content in my thoughts to imagine a man, a dad to those boys, who had that big heart from his Momma with love for all and a heart for forgiveness. Certainly, I owed him that much from our brief encounter. After all, we'd talked shrimp and crab boils and not presidential politics. All I knew at this point was a young man from Macon had two fine sons and a job interview that might well change his life from whatever it was to a life in a mostly white city. I hoped he was ready for that if that's what he wanted or needed. I, of course, couldn't know which it was.

After Miles and I retired, we started a regular schedule of going to the Daisy Cafe Tuesday through Friday. Perhaps since we had walked away from the church, walking to this cafe served for us as a kind of community. Like the church, it had its welcoming folk and those who would remain distant despite years of proximity from booth to table. Miles and I had our regular spot where I sat looking towards the door and he across the booth. After his death, I saw no point in changing a comfortable pattern.

And comfortable, I became. Some mornings were simply, "Sausage?"—not even a "good morning." Maggie was the more talkative of the two but she and Ethel both appreciated those rare mornings when the place was as quiet as it was some mornings. On those mornings, even the ol' boys' just sat quietly drinking their coffee. It never took Noel long to get my breakfast done, and time allowing, he'd fry up a couple eggs for himself and join me in the booth.

He was a hard working man. Originally from Guam, a descendant of the Chamorros who inhabited the island for 4000 years. The indigenous people knew all manner of hardship as their history was rife with devastation both from mother nature and occupying forces. When 400 years of Spanish rule gave way to American rule, the islanders soon enough found themselves in a new horror. Soon after Pearl Harbor, the Japanese occupied the island for thirty-one months and inflicted forced labor, forced prostitution, set up concentration camps and carried out executions.

While before his time, the occupation left its mark on his family. Several died, more were brutalized and two of his aunts raised half-Japanese children from the sexual abuse they sustained from the soldiers. There would be no way to shield these children from the reality of their conception, but the family's respect for life ensured as much dignity for the children as was conceivable under the circumstances.

During the Vietnam era, the US used agent orange as a common herbicide near their bases. Like the people of other US territories, the islanders have no real political voice in their own destiny. Uncle Sam is happy to have them as military recruits but in return denies them a vote in presidential elections, a voting representative in Congress, and basic federal benefits stateside citizens take for granted. All this to say, if your family has made it this far, you had to be both strong and lucky. I always thought it explained how hard Noel worked as well as how effectively he seemed to take all things in stride.

His family was Catholic like most families on Guam. The Jesuits first brought the religion to the island and little has happened to diversify it from those roots those centuries ago. Noel's maternal grandmother "never missed a mass" according to Noel. If the priest was celebrating any day of the week no matter the hour, she would be there. Noel's parents were little more than Sunday-only Catholics, and Noel had become the decidedly only-for-funerals Catholic; but he did like to go to midnight mass on Christmas Eve, more as a way to celebrate his own birthday than the Christ child's perhaps.

Like many of the islanders he was fluent in Chamorro, Filipino and English. You could always tell when he was in a cussin' mood because you'd hear what we all assumed was Chamorro coming from the kitchen. He'd also work a choice word here and there into his English conversation. It was easy enough in those cases to guess what word had been selected for substitution.

His family was poor and Noel went to work full time when he was sixteen. Eventually, he got a GED but never had any dreams of going to college. He couldn't have remained still long enough for that kind of learning. He could only bear to sit with me at any one time for maybe five minutes before he'd be thinking of something back in the kitchen that he ought to be doing. The owners of the Daisy Cafe had a good thing, and they knew it. He was as loyal, honest and thrifty as they come. I have no idea what they paid him though I'm sure it should be more. He was never going to ask for anything. All he knew was work, and he was a fine cook. Captain Parker, whose mother, Daisy, started the cafe had been stationed in Guam and had made a career in the Navy. He saw how hard Noel worked at the restaurant near the base, and knowing his mother was about worn out from running the cafe, offered to bring Noel over to the states and let him take it over. They talked terms which took, according to Noel, about 10 minutes to agree to, and within the month Noel was on his first plane ride to his new life.

He didn't even bother to tell his family he was going. He had an independent streak that ran deep and with eight brothers and three sisters he figured there were plenty to take care of his parents. And he reckoned those brothers and sisters would miss him about as much as he'd miss them.

"I'm a middle child," he explained soon after he arrived, "And how many middle children have you met that anyone ever takes note of? My mother named me Noel because I was born on Christmas day. Because of that, they all at least knew my birthday which is more than I could say about me remembering any of theirs."

Work would take precedent over relationships. In Guam, while still in his twenties, he'd already been married and divorced twice. In the states he'd use his day off to cavort somewhere with someone but where and with whom he'd never say. He only took one day off a week—Mondays. The one day the cafe was closed. His only back-up plan was Maggie's husband, Bob.

Bob was the short order cook for Daisy and retired early when she retired. Noel liked to say he could do the work of two since he replaced both Daisy and Bob in the kitchen. The truth is, he did do the work of two. Bob didn't mind the occasional fill-in if needed—front or back of the house, but in reality he was content that the three mainstays rarely needed any fill-in help.

Noel lived in one of two apartments above the cafe. I can imagine it's spotless just like the downstairs. Some old diners and cafes have a layer of grease that permeates the walls, ceilings and

turn down a salary twice what he's worth to have the opportunity you can provide.'"

The boys looked up at their daddy with their mouths hanging open—perhaps it was them thinking their dad gave up a chance for a big job in Atlanta for their sake. Whatever was going through their minds, Tyler was fixed on them as Mr. Cross told of the old boss's recommendation. It was all he could muster to keep from getting glassy-eyed which he was despite the effort.

Tyler put both hands together in front of his mouth as though he was about to utter a prayer, and with a sigh he summed up the emotion running through him at that moment, "I'm overwhelmed."

After lunch, the four returned to the car and headed back to city hall. Tyler mentioned the couple of realtors he thought he would contact in his housing search while in town. Offering one possible option Mr. Cross said, "I don't know that this will be a suitable solution for you or that an offer to rent will be made, but I happen to know that your breakfast companion has the other half of his duplex empty at the moment. He'd rather have it sit empty as it has for several months now than have a tenant he wants to get rid of after they've moved in. If a bit smaller than you might want, you will find it immaculate, and it's right in town and handy to everything."

Tyler, reflecting on how the day had progressed so far shook his head, "If that did work out, I'd have to say today is set to become the most extraordinary day of my life."

Chapter Four

Mr. Cross delivered them back to city hall and excused himself as he needed to get to an appointment. Before leaving he gave Tyler the phone number and address for "Mr. August." "You tell him John Cross suggested he was the best place to start on a rental search. He might know of something open on short notice. That'll give him a chuckle. He retires early but isn't one for taking naps. You don't have to worry about calling him any time of the day when you get the chance."

Lisa got all the paperwork in order and sat down with Tyler and Mayor Wilson to go over everything. A start date of one month from then was agreed upon, the salary and benefits all signed off on officially in an offer and acceptance letter and their business was concluded. The boys thanked Lisa for the puzzle, and Johnny said he expected her to finish it for them. She said she would. Tyler noticed that the puzzle of summer flowers had one area completely filled in and worked out from there. It was the daisies.

Tyler debated whether to drive by first and scope out my duplex, talk with a relator or just call and see what I had to say. He decided on a hybrid approach. He would drive by my duplex, and if nothing put him off about the neighborhood, he'd try to reach me on the phone. Then if I didn't answer or he didn't feel right about the neighborhood or the duplex, he'd stop in at one of the realtors he'd already scoped out as having a number of rentals. The day was moving quickly so he figured the soonest he'd be looking at a place was well into the next day or even later. They would have to head back to Macon by Sunday at the latest.

When he got to the car he phoned his boss to give him the news. It wasn't until then that the boss let on that he'd had the call with Mr. Cross. "So they took my advice, I see," was his reaction to the news. "You've given me fair warning that you were looking. If you want to stick to the two week's notice we discussed, I'll count from today."

"We agreed I'd start here in a month so if I can get at least full a week or so to get moved, that would be great."

"You got it. Shoot me an email when you get a chance to make it all official and put whatever day you want as your official last day."

"I'll send that this evening when I get back to the hotel," Tyler said.

"Congratulations, Tyler. I'm very happy for you if sad for Macon."

"Thank you, sir. I'll be in touch."

Tyler drove by and saw me out in the yard with Penny-girl trailing behind me on the leash. My back was to the street and only she turned to look at the passing car. Tyler was sure I had not seen them drive by.

The boys spotted me. "Hey, there's Mr. August," they said in unison.

Tyler liked the look of the neighborhood and went to the corner, turned and called me giving me a couple minutes to get back in the house where I was clearly headed with the dog. "Mr. August, this is Tyler Jemison. John Cross gave me your phone number. My interview went well and the city of Boone has offered me the job as city manager. He suggested I might ask you if you were aware of any rentals that might be available in short order."

Mr. Cross was correct. I did chuckle. "John thought I might know of rentals to be had, huh? Well, I might know of at least one sitting empty at the moment. It's only two bedrooms but it does have a small office and two baths so a small family might work. I should warn you though that the landlord is persnickety about who his tenants are. Still think you might be interested in taking a look?"

"Yes, sir, we would."

I then said, "I suspect John Cross has already given you the address of this vacant rental. Am I correct about that?"

"Yes, he has," Tyler said.

"And he's warned you about that landlord?"

"Warned wouldn't be the right word," Tyler responded, adding, "It was more something along the line of a good man wanting to ensure good neighbors."

I said, "I can see they hired you in part for your diplomatic skills. You want to come over now?"

"If it's convenient," Tyler responded.

"It is. And if I were you I would have already driven by so you are probably close enough to be here before two shakes of a lamb's tail. Would that be the case?"

Tyler said, "It is indeed."

"Head over here then," and I hung-up.

I was sitting on the small front porch of my part of the duplex when the boys pulled up. I motioned them to head directly to the vacant side and I headed that way as well, arriving at the front door just as they stepped onto the porch.

"I'm delighted to hear the interview went well. Did these two cause a ruckus at city hall? I hope they didn't have to be locked up in the jail while you were being interviewed."

The boys got a big kick out of that. Johnny said, "No, we worked on a puzzle, but jail might have been more fun."

From what Mr. Cross had said, Tyler was expecting a spotless, well-cared-for but empty apartment. What he hadn't expected was stepping into a *Southern Living* fully furnished dream home. This was no ordinary duplex apartment. It was a timber frame gem that immediately reminded him of his Uncle Ira and Aunt Ruby's own timber frame. Tyler also immediately thought his new salary, while good, was not going to cover the likes of this place.

"Mr. August, this is beautiful, but before we traipse through it, I have to say I'm sure we can't afford it. And I'm equally sure you don't want a young family staying in it."

The boys' eyes were as big as saucers which did not escape my notice. It was clear they'd never seen anything furnished quite to this standard. Neither one of them made a sound.

I proceeded as though I'd not heard anything Tyler said. "Let me show you the rest of the house." We went from room to room as I opened every closet door, showing them the bathrooms, the first bedroom with two twin beds, the second with a king and taking them into the backyard where there was a large patio—half covered with a large gas grill, beautiful trees and a fountain which I turned on as we went into the yard. To Tyler's surprise there were even two swings hanging from an old beech in the back corner of the yard. It was all enclosed with a cedar fence. I didn't say a word but rather wandered slowly around the yard as to give them leave to do the same. Then I headed back into the kitchen.

Inside Tyler said, "I half expected Jacques Pepin to be in the kitchen when we came back in here. A gourmet chef is the only thing I haven't seen. And you really rent this out?"

"I do when the spirit moves me which it must be said isn't often—especially of late. You interested?" I asked.

The boys were out back on the swings. Tyler pondered the appropriate response, "I've got some good boys as you've already said you believed to be the case, but you don't want two boys and their daddy living here. I can't imagine why you ever would. And I'm certain the rent is more than I can afford."

I motioned for Tyler to sit at the dining room table as I did the same. The bright sunlight flooded through the picture window. Just beyond was the side garden which was profuse with roses in bloom. Unintentionally, I had framed the composition so that the sunlight looked like a halo around my head. It was my intention that Tyler was facing out to the rose garden.

This old man started in. "I'm not a great believer in signs, but I also know what God puts in front of you, only a fool looks the other way. Too many can't see the beauty in front of them, and fewer still know how to express gratitude when they should be bubblin' up with it non-stop like that fountain out there.

"Did we meet by chance this morning? Did the city council, who takes a month of Sundays to make a decision, suddenly lose all sense of restraint today? Did John Cross, who I've known for going on thirty years, just happen to mention a landlord who keeps an empty apartment for when the spirit moves him? All coincidences I'm sure. Nothing to do with the spirit of Momma Daisy up there thumping us over the head to be sure we know what we've got in front of us. It's pretty clear to me that this old man, that city council and Mayor all got the message loud and clear. If you are a no account, trashy such and such, you've done a masterful job of fooling us. I'm as sure as anything that you are the real deal, and it's for the old to help the young.

"Now here is the deal—whatever you got that you want to bring here from Macon, I'll move out whatever needs to be moved out. If you want to sell everything you've got and move here with the place as is, then that's fine too. It's just stuff. I'm not preserving it as a museum. That it happens to be nice stuff is just a matter of fact. It's still just stuff.

"As to the rent, I'm pretty sure you can afford it. All utilities are paid. Internet is provided. I never wanted to go through the hassle of turning them on and off as people moved out. The place has been empty now two years which even for me is a new record though barely so. That's a long way of saying I don't care about the money, but I know you'd only feel right paying a reasonable rent. So, how does five hundred a month sound?"

Tyler said, "It sounds to me like that's undervalued by about three times, even if it was empty and not furnished like Michael Greer just stepped out to go to the grocery store."

"Well, your fellow Georgian did have good taste, and the fact that you know who he is suggests you have an appreciation for things crafted with care. So, maybe I've overpriced the place and it should be four hundred instead of five."

Tyler laughed and said, "I think you took that in the wrong direction."

"If you want to take tomorrow and see what else is out, feel free to do so. If you want to go home and think about it, that's fine too. I'm not fixin' to rent it out from under you. That said, it's near the boys' school, and they've already settled into those swings out there. I'm going back to my apartment. You and the boys spend whatever time you want here, and let the front door lock when you leave. You can knock on my door, call later today or in the coming days whenever you decide, or I suppose I could never hear from you again though I doubt you'd leave things that way. Some would. And yes, you talked me down to four hundred. Take it or leave it."

As I headed to the door I stopped to say, "Oh, one last thing. When Miles and I moved to Boone we didn't bring much with us. You might consider doing the same."

I realized at that point Tyler didn't know who Miles was, but I figured the last thing I owed him in his decision was the fact that there was no Mrs. August in the picture now or before.

Tyler went into the backyard with the boys. They moved back into the house and did a slow look around the apartment. They sat down in the living room. Tyler asked the boys, "Johnny, Jimmy, Mr. August has offered us this home. Would you boys like to live here, or should we look at some other places and then decide?"

Jimmy offered the only sensible reply, "There are daisies in the backyard. Momma wants us here."

Tyler had seen them too, but hadn't paid much attention to them until Jimmy called them out. He thought it was too early for daisies to be in bloom, but he had seen a few in the large bed already blooming. His rational mind told him it must have been an early warm spring. His heart told him some other hand was at work.

"Well, I'm gonna let you tell Mr. August that," he said to Jimmy, and they went, and Jimmy knocked on the old man's door.

Chapter Five

I was happy they'd decided to stay next door and had given them the key and my email address. When they decided what they might be bringing up from Macon, they were to let me know so I could arrange the apartment as needs be. With more settled than Tyler ever imagined possible in the two days since they arrived, he decided to head back to Macon the next day. Before they left town, we agreed to meet for breakfast at the Daisy Cafe.

They arrived in their shiny red RAV4 just as I was walking up. We entered the cafe together and immediately proceeded to our "usual table." Each sat in the same seat they had the morning before. I said to Tyler, "Seems we've all found our particular place in the pew."

Maggie approached the table with two coffees in hand and set them down before us as she mixed greeting and duty, "Good morning, fine sirs. I didn't expect to see the four of you all in here again this morning. Do you want to see a menu or do you already know what you want?"

Johnny, who had copied my order of bacon and eggs, asked what I was having this morning.

"By way of celebration for your new situation in Boone, I think I'll treat myself to a mushroom Swiss omelette and, with that, I must have a side of good crispy bacon. That probably doesn't sound as good to you as a waffle and sausage. What do you think?"

Johnny thought it did apparently, "Ms. Maggie, I'll have what Mr. August is having."

Jimmy piped up, "I'll have the waffle."

"No sausage?" Maggie asked.

"No, Ms. Maggie, just the waffle and syrup."

Tyler ordered the drinks for them, "Orange juice for both boys. No Coke this morning. Johnny will get his Coke when we are on the road back to Macon. I'll have the omelette as well with a side of sausage."

"Leaving Boone so soon?" Maggie asked.

I picked things up from here. "Maggie," I said all this loud enough for the ol' boys' table to hear since I could see they were tuned into whatever was going on at our table anyway. "I'm pleased to introduce you to the new city manager, Mr. Tyler Jemison. You already know the boys. They will be moving into my duplex."

She said, "Well, congratulations! That duplex has been empty so long I'm surprised you could get through the cobwebs over the front door."

"I thank you," Tyler said. "And I suspect you know this gentleman well enough that a spider would be making a big mistake trying to settle anywhere on that duplex. It stands ready for a photo shoot at any time."

"Except I wouldn't let any photographers in there," I added.

Maggie was off to update Noel and Ethel on the big news. Ethel had missed all this as she was back loading the dishwasher. She came scurrying out still in her waterproof apron to congratulate Tyler on the job and me finally having a tenant again.

Noel stuck his head out the kitchen door long enough to say, "Hey, congratulations. Breakfast is on the Daisy today!" Turning to the ol' boys' table and any others within earshot he clarified. "Just August's table. The rest of you don't get any ideas." With that he was back to work.

We had our very satisfactory breakfast, and I knew they would be eager to get started on the long drive back to Macon. We'd have plenty of time to visit once they were settled here. When they finished I suggested, "You best skedaddle. You've got a lot of miles to cover."

Tyler got up, shook my hand and waved his hands for the boys to head to the door. "We'll see you soon."

"Yup," was all I said and gave them a final wave.

With the Jemisons' departure, the ol' boys' table took up the topic of city hiring. The general consensus seemed to be wrapped in the first ol' boy expressing it loud enough to be sure it was heard by everyone in the Daisy Cafe. "Apparently, the city council doesn't think anybody in North Carolina can run the city for them. They have to bring in someone from Macon."

Never-shy Maggie, though it did seem to me I should have piped in to preserve the piddly tips the ol' boys' table generally left, said also loud enough for all to hear, "That last North Carolina boy worked out real well. Born and raised in Boone and stole three hundred thousand."

While I'm sure it had little to do with coming from outside the State and a whole lot to do with a black man getting the job, at least Maggie's forthright truth shut the ol' boys down. At least for the moment. One quickly deflected to a new topic, the weather, generally safe as long as the words "climate change" were avoided.

I had put myself about thirty minutes ahead of my usual schedule to accommodate the boys getting on the road that morning. As they left, I picked up my near-empty cup and moved over to my "favorite pew," the booth in the back corner opposite the kitchen door. Through the door came John Cross, heading straight to me. He saw Ethel, and in his usual command and control voice said, "Coffee, Ethel." As I'd have done to him as well, no permission was asked or required—he sat down in the booth across from me. Years of familiarity if not actual friendship afforded each of us this presumption of welcome.

"Morning, John." He was not a regular at the cafe though not entirely infrequent. I suspected he was there to talk about Tyler. I was tempted to what little mischief an old man can have at this stage of life.

He avoided small talk and got right to it. He was always a man with a schedule and nothing was to interfere with that. "I understand you met a young man here at the cafe recently, Tyler Jemison."

"Tyler...Tyler Jemison." I wrinkled my brow as best I could in deep thought. "Name doesn't ring a bell."

"A man with two small boys. Said he had breakfast with you here at the cafe. I thought he said it was just yesterday morning."

"Oh, them. Yea, the place was unusually packed yesterday, and my booth was taken. The four of us ended up at the table by the kitchen door. Seemed like nice enough boys. Quiet, which I always like. They weren't from around here as I recall."

"The story as I heard it was you were in a choir that sang in their church and you even remembered their grandmother."

"I guess we did talk about my one trip to Macon. How did you meet them?"

"Tyler applied for the city manager job, and we offered it to him."

"That's nice."

"And maybe I misread your interest in Tyler and his boys for which you will have to forgive me. I came here this morning to let you know you might get a call from him today. I said you were a good place to start for a possible rental. He was planning on taking the next couple days to begin looking for a place. I thought I ought to get here to let you know. I told Tyler you are usually back home around 10:00."

I wasn't quite ready to give it up just yet. "And you thought, as picky as you know I am about who lives in that duplex, that I'd want a father with two boys living there. Did you ask—are they going to be coming here with a pack of Great Danes to kennel in the backyard and two or three house cats to climb the curtains?"

Maggie and Ethel were both trying to stay tuned in as they went about their work. They never topped off coffee cups as much as they did then. John even looked at them with some curiosity as to why his cup couldn't get the slightest chance of cooling down.

Between the growing grins from Maggie and Ethel and my exaggerations, he was finally clueing in on my deception.

He said, "You sack of shit—he's already called you, hasn't he? And you've already said he could stay there at least until he found something more permanent, haven't ya? You're gonna leave here to meet them, show it and decide for sure."

I came back with, "You think you worked it all out and you haven't. No, I am not meeting them later to show it to them. We did all that yesterday right after they left city hall. And no, they won't be staying there until they find something better. They will be staying there as long as it all works out, which I hope is a long time."

John grinned. "You old fart. Well, you have to admit this about you and me. We both saw something in that young man and those two boys that made us want to do good for them."

I grinned right back at him. "John Cross, whatever anybody says, I always knew you were a good judge of character. How I balance that with you calling me an old fart and a sack of shit is another matter. I guess I have to accept you might well be right."

37

"Well, August Kibler, you also know how to take a tiny bit of bait and reel in a big fish." Nodding his head toward Ethel and Maggie, he added, "Your two accomplices over there who clearly knew the truth might agree you're an old fart, but they, like me, would also say you're a friend and a damn fine one at that. And anybody who keeps to the right side of wrong is gonna find as generous a man as there is in this town."

Huh! A friend. Not sure what final comeback I expected, but that one did surprise me. To have the last word before he was off to the next meeting I said, "John, this town is in good hands. If there is one person we should ever give a lifetime integrity award to, it should be you. And knowing your father for the short time I did, I know you honor that fine man."

He stood, put out his hand and held mine more than shook it. I could see conjuring up his father's memory was about to make the command-and-control councilman emotional. He let loose my hand, and without a word turned moving towards the door as he gave us a backward wave.

I picked up my cup for one last sip and muttered softly to myself, "Bless you, my friend."

Part II

Chapter Six

Miles and I were both in the choir in Anderson. We'd both been to that Macon church all those years ago, though I had never asked him if he had the same vivid memories about the church as I had held onto all these years. It must be confessed, we also fell in love during that trip and that Sunday morning in Macon was when we both realized such was the case. This wasn't news we were inclined to share with anyone. There was a fairly open group at the college but, being poster children for the "out" community was not something either of us was ready to inflict on my Mennonite parents or Miles' Catholic father. His mother's family was Church of God which is how he ended up at Anderson, but he was raised Catholic. Fortunately for me at the time, our Swiss conservatism leaned very heavily on not having to talk about things personal. Miles' Cajun roots—he was born and raised in Franklin, Louisiana—were a lot more public shall we say. We'd talked about going to Louisiana after we graduated. This was mostly my idea. On one trip to New Orleans we took our junior year, I had acquired a love of Louisiana cookin'. Miles had his mother's gumbo recipe, and we feasted on that year round.

When we moved from Indiana to Baton Rouge where I would start graduate school at LSU and where he had secured a job as a programmer, he soon enough told his family about us. It appeared to me a mixed bag. His mother had died while we were both in Anderson and his father seemed mostly unfazed by the revelation. I gathered he wasn't really surprised.

His brothers were another matter. They'd act fine with it one time and then use it as some way to demean him when in the mood. Once his dad died and we'd moved to North Carolina, the distant miles made it all easier. He would talk on the phone for long periods of time with each of them, but they weren't ever on our vacation travel plans. The boys got all together the last time after their dad's funeral, when the oldest turned 70 and his kids organized a big Bergeron family reunion. After the reunion Miles said, "There, we've got that done and don't need to go back to Louisiana on my account unless you want to dump me in the Bayou Teche."

I said, "If you don't mind, I'll keep you here with me and the dogs."

I never hid our relationship from my family. They met Miles while we were still in college. My parents liked Miles a lot. Back in those days we would sing duets together, and we had a rather inspiring version of *Jesus Paid it All* from an arrangement that Hale and Wilder had done, which we sang one Sunday at Park Place when my parents were visiting. We did several of their songs over the years.

Years later, when we joined the Episcopal church, for whatever reason, we no longer were asked to sing duets. Those type special numbers didn't seem to fit into liturgical worship as it did with the Church of God that we attended both in Anderson and in Louisiana.

I thought the Midwest was hot in the summer, but that first summer in Baton Rouge I thought I'd died and gone to hell. What was I thinking wanting to come here? The native Cajun I lived with had a natural temper as it was, and as the heat and humidity cranked up so did his temper. It would be the roughest years of our co-joined life, but neither of us had any notion that this was something to be discarded as a result of the Louisiana heat. I was determined to stay put until I finished my degree, and the fact that I worked part-time (though nearly full-time, truth be told) while working on my degree out in the heat only made my love of the deep south that much less authentic and me all the more eager to escape at the first opportunity.

One summer we flew to Asheville. We'd both wanted to go to Biltmore. What a place! And even in the dead of summer we felt like we'd died and gone to heaven. The hellish-heat of Louisiana was behind us for a few days before reality would take us back. I said to Miles, "When I'm finishing up I think we need to both start looking at options in this direction." When we got back home we began in earnest to find what colleges and universities there were anywhere in the north Georgia to West Virginia mountains. I wasn't a whole lot more fond of months of gray and cold as I'd known growing up in the Midwest than I was of Louisiana hellheat, so I wasn't keen on venturing too far north. And as one of my uncles once said of green beans—he loved them far away—I rather loved most of my family in the same fashion.

We more or less easily transitioned from Park Place Church in Anderson to our Church of God congregation in Baton Rouge. Less easily than more as the months progressed. We were both in the choir and we were instantly big hits with our voices. But the Church-a-god was a changin'. They'd started singling out the Augusts and Mileses of the church to make it clear we were not to be in any leadership position. That the new directive within the denomination happened right as we graduated from Anderson really threw us for a loop. It had been what would be called later "don't ask, don't tell" up to that point. Now it seemed they would be overturning rocks trying to find who was doing what with whom. It was all too obvious that our minister was cheering all this on. There were plenty of faculty at Anderson who were as appalled as we were at the direction. Some faculty left. Some left before they knew they'd be escorted to the door when some less-friendly administration took over from the power changes going on inside the greater church. It was our general observation that so long as you were willing to lie, you were good to advance to their so-called "positions of leadership." If you were honest, you were out. We both had our first real reckoning that we needed to leave.

We had a neighbor who went to the Episcopal church. He and his wife taught Miles and me how to play bridge. We got to be close friends and decided to wander in unannounced to one of the services. Neither one of us knew much about the church. He'd answered a few basics for us. The church had an early service without music which he always attended, and a later one with music. Naturally, we opted for the later service with music.

It was quite an experience for this Mennonite-Church of God boy; it was less so for the Catholic reared Miles. The bell was rung several times. Then a great cloud of smoke came wafting down the aisle with a teenager swinging the fire-pot, (I would later learn as the thurible), twirling it around a great circle with his right hand, followed by two smaller children carrying "torches," followed by another teenager holding up a large brass cross, followed by a man and a woman wearing white robes, followed by another man with a robe and a stole worn diagonally across his chest, followed finally by the priest who was dressed in a great cope that looked to me like something Scarlet O'Hara had pulled down off the dining room windows and stitched-up for the man.

Once up front, he took the fire-pot and made circles around, up and over the altar with the smoke billowing out. He then handed it back to the boy, who flung it three times at the congregation before finally hanging if off to the side. It wouldn't be long until it was restocked with incense and brought back down the aisle for the one with the diagonal stole to read from the assigned Gospel for the day.

We had certainly walked into what we learned later was referred to as a "high church" parish. I can't say the sermon was up to the Church of God standards that we'd heard at Park Place on Sundays or in campus chapel, but what it lacked in substance it made up for in brevity.

However, in full disclosure, there were exceptions to the usual good sermons at Park Place. One in particular stood out to us. Just when a friend of ours, several years older than Miles and me, Frederica, was going through a troublesome divorce, the sermon was on the theme of "what the world needs is more guilt." Well, I suppose for some aspect of empire that would be true enough, but for the lambs in his care, it well missed the mark that Sunday! In the "all things work together for good" department, that divorce brought her closer to us in a friendship that was lasting. She had a beautiful lyrical voice and over the years I often find myself closing my eyes and hearing her sing to me.

I had gone with Miles to mass in Anderson a couple of times, but compared to this, it would have to be described as ho-hum. We both preferred Park Place for the music it offered. It suited both of us to a "t." This "high church" had a good organ and we liked the hymns. They had an okay choir up in the balcony with the organ. It was a pretty church and had some similar look on the outside to the Episcopal church in Anderson. I'd always been a little curious even then but never wandered in.

We were invited back by several to join them for coffee in the parish hall which we politely declined. When we got in the car, Miles was the first to say something. "Now that was church! It reminded me of the old Catholic mass in Franklin before the guitars came in and ruined it."

I said, "Wow. I might even like the incense if I could actually breathe and sing. If we ever go back, we are not sitting on the aisle again."

Over bridge the next Saturday, we told our friends we'd gone to the later service the Sunday before. When we recounted the billows of smoke he laughed and said, "Ten-thirty is high church. We eight-o'clockers are low church." He wondered if we'd go back. We did the next day and every Sunday after that.

Between my work and school schedule and the overtime that Miles put in, neither of us wanted to get too attached to this group. We weren't planning to be around that long. We attended every Sunday sitting on the "Gospel side" over by the wall so we could breathe and sing at the same time, and we stayed for coffee in the parish hall about half the time. Beyond that, we skipped such things as the annual meeting and never bothered getting "received" as they would have with Miles being a Catholic or "confirmed" as they would require a Mennonite-Church of God'er to do. I never did reconcile the difference in my mind why my background required some extra step of instruction and confirmation, but one thing you have to say regarding Episcopalians—rules are rules! It was pretty clear from the first sermon to the last that I was far more clued in on scripture than the good reverend. I owed that to instruction as a Mennonite child—but even more to an Old Testament professor at Anderson who actually made me interested in the Old Testament. With his instruction came the wise counsel, "Please go to church, but never check your mind at the door." For now we stuck to the notion we both preferred from the Church of God. No membership required. One day I would relent and be confirmed and Miles received. We would become "church members." And we would come to know more than one priest and bishop who would have preferred the two of us had checked our minds at the door.

Chapter Seven

It took me five years to finally finish that blasted MBA, mostly due to my work schedule. I had little choice. I had left Anderson with too much debt having gone to a private college and was determined to not go any deeper. Thanks to Miles' advancement to analyst, we were doing pretty well, and my loan was paid the same month I graduated from LSU. I would continue toiling under the hot sun until one of us had an opportunity to move both of us to mountains. That was our hope at least. It wasn't necessarily harder to get a job in those days, but it certainly was harder to know what was available if you weren't in the neighborhood. Websites were not yet a thing. We took a two-prong approach to our job search. One, we would each send a cover letter and resume to every college and university we found in the higher education directory at the LSU library. Second, we would take as much vacation time as possible to that area and just go from one to the next to see first hand the place and visit their HR offices. If anything looked promising, we'd follow up until they told us to get lost.

We had an encouraging prospect in Boone, North Carolina. The university was looking for an analyst who knew the systems that Miles already knew—they were getting ready to start a new implementation—and they had a posting for an assistant director of the physical plant. What I lacked in years' experience in that exact job posting, I hoped I might overcome with having the preferred degree they were seeking and plenty of practical construction experience. We applied and went back to Baton Rouge. In a couple weeks, Miles had a phone interview and they scheduled an onsite. We drove back up for the interview.

In those days the computers were huge and the memory to operate them was minuscule by later standards. Programmers like Miles were the baling wire and chewing gum that made clunky systems work at all. In his five years at LSU he had automated a lot of HR and finance operations. Out of boredom he learned all he could about the registrar's office. He had been awarded an outstanding achievement award for his efforts. I thought he would be a shoo-in if he got the chance to interview. He interviewed. We waited. Two weeks later he had a job offer. Three weeks after that

44

we were on our way to Boone. One month from his interview we had an apartment and he was on the payroll.

The physical plant, if they were moving at all on my application, was moving at a snail's pace. I kept following up as much as was reasonable to do, and got the same answer each time. "We are still reviewing applicants." I did let them know my address had changed and was now in Boone. I hoped this might give me a little edge over more far-flung applicants. Finally, they called to set up an interview.

It was really quite uneventful. The director interviewed me by himself and then passed me onto three others, one at a time, who asked the same questions, clearly working from a script. It was impossible to tell where any one of them might particularly be lining me up as far as interviewees were concerned. There was no effort to try to sell me on working for the university, which I assumed was a bad sign. I left quite discouraged and decided I would look for a job as a project manager for some contractor. Over the next two weeks I applied at the three that seemed to have the most promise and an immediate opening. Two scheduled interviews. One called to offer me a job ten minutes after I had hung up with the university HR office who had offered me the job in the physical plant. I was shocked, but immediately accepted. I told the contractor, Bill Cross (John's father), of the job offer I'd just accepted a few minutes earlier, and his only comment was perhaps he should have gotten around to calling that morning. I thanked him—he thanked me, and that was that.

Upon arriving in Boone, we didn't have to think too long about a church. We found an Episcopal church we thought looked pretty good to us, gave it a try or two, visited the Lutherans a couple times to validate or alter our intent and stuck with the plan.

The Episcopal church we attended had a nice organ but not much of a choir. We were a lot more inclined to usher than join the choir though Miles was asked on numerous occasions to serve as cantor for one thing or another. The two most frequent were chanting the Exultant at the Great Vigil of Easter and the Great Litany the first Sunday of Advent and two Sundays each year during Lent. There was no curate, and the priest couldn't carry a

45

tune to save his life. I will always contend that two things propelled him towards those who wanted him to be ordained—his rich voice chanting the services so beautifully and his ability to "mourn with those who mourn."

Once the church learned I could keep books, they didn't care if I could sing or not. They needed a treasurer, and I was willing to do it. As things went over time, I was really treasurer and other jack-of-all trades. If a big meal was needed, I was called. If something didn't work, I was called. I don't know why, since I was never junior or senior warden, and the only committee I ever led was the stewardship committee. You can probably begin to see the pattern. If no one wanted to do it, ask August. Once between priests, I even planned the Christmas eve service which included a fairly impressive worship folder so all the visitors could easily follow along. The cover included a very colorful and somewhat abstract nativity scene by the artist He Qi who I contacted to get his approval for reprinting it which he graciously accommodated. There were carols, scriptures and poems. I lined up different readers for each scripture and each poem. Miles memorized "Eddi's Service." He was the only one who went so far as to memorize their part, including me. It really was a beautiful service. Just stating fact. Every year at home, I would remind Miles that I wanted to hear him recite "Eddi." Some years he would. Some he wouldn't. To this day, I've never heard anyone recite it as well as he did. It always brought me to tears. I'm certain Kipling couldn't have done it better himself. What spoke so powerfully to us from this poem was its absolute inclusion. The old priest was mocked by his fellow Saxons, but as he would say, "I dare not shut His chapel on such as care to attend."

But I digress. That Christmas eve program seemed to set the standard for church bulletins, and I found myself as layout and print master as well as accountant, cook and bottle washer right up until the time we parted company.

Both of us loved having projects to work on. This suited both our jobs well, but it also served to propel us towards building a place where we could finally get a couple dogs and call home. We wasted no time after arriving in Boone. We found a deep empty lot on the northwest side of town—almost two acres. I would have liked to have been further out, but being on call as I was 24/7 it just wasn't practical to get too far flung. Our idea was to have the frame constructed by a contractor, hire an electrician and plumber and do the rest ourselves. My grandfather had built many barns—timber frame, mortise and tenon. We both loved timber frames, and so I set out to design a duplex to give us some investment income with the idea that we would live on one side and rent the other. Since children were nowhere in the plan, we agreed to each unit being two bed, two bath. The rental side would be for adults only. We hoped 55+, but knew we would likely have to compromise on that.

Plans done, financing in place, contractors and subs hired, we broke ground on June 1. We moved into our half of the duplex one week before Christmas and had the other side finished by the end of March. We were both so excited to be in and put up our first Christmas tree. We also gave ourselves two golden retriever pups for Christmas, who lost no time chewing off a corner of a new oriental rug we had purchased for the living room.

Miles had not seen the gift that one or both of the pups had given us. I heard from the kitchen, "Oh, aren't you just the cutest puppy ever!" I could see Miles at one of the breakfast table chairs with the male puppy, Jem, in his lap as the puppy proceeded to throw-up rug all over him. "What is this?" he screamed as much at me as the dog.

I said, "Oh that's the cutest little puppy in the world throwing up your new oriental rug."

No need to repeat the words that followed. Suffice it to say, the ragin' Cajun was not happy.

Chapter Eight

Knowing Baton Rouge was a stopping point and not the destination, we had rented while there and kept our "stuff" to what would fit in a towable U-Haul. This was not an easy thing for us. We both were eager to start a real home—well-built and well-furnished, however modest it might be. Now that the duplex was done, our humble few items looked pretty pathetic. We bought that rug and two nice chairs which we put on each side of the fireplace. We didn't worry about the empty apartment next door. As far as investments go, that one was off to what would prove to be a long pattern of sitting empty. Not for lack of interest, but lack of suitable neighbors we would be interested in.

There was a young man who was interviewing in the same department as Miles and if offered a job, would be looking for a place to settle as he was moving to Boone from Charlotte. He appeared with Miles one evening.

"This is Robert Stiles. He interviewed for the open position today. I thought we might show him the apartment."

I'm not the jealous type, but the young man's good looks did give me a little pause as to Miles' motives. I said, "I hope you're not looking for anything furnished. We don't have a stick of furniture in the apartment."

"No," he said, "I have my own furniture."

I wanted to know the state of his employment. "So they offered you the job then?"

Miles piped in, "No, this is just exploratory."

I'd never heard Miles phrase anything quite that way but proceeded to lead the way over to the apartment. I think he expected the apartment side to be a cheap version of our side. When he saw it was identical in finish if not the exact layout he was blown away. "This is so lovely!"

I thought to myself, do straight men use the word lovely? In North Carolina? Yea, probably not. I said, "Miles and I love the joinery of timber frames. We just love sitting in a chair and staring at the timbers. It occurs to me I've been a terrible Episcopalian. I haven't offered you a drink. Can I get you something while you and Miles look around?" I already knew what Miles would have if we were drinking.

"I wouldn't turn something down," he responded.

I listed a few options. "Martini? Wine? Scotch? Bloody Mary? G&T?" I figured that was enough to suggest we had a stocked bar but not to wander into something too complex.

"A gin martini on the rocks would be great."

"I'm off to my duties," I said and went back over to our apartment.

I was just setting the glasses on a tray when the two reappeared in the apartment. "Here you go. One Beefeater martini for each of us with olives. Hope that's okay."

"Great!," Robert responded with a grin. Holding up his glass, "Cheers!"

Robert was a few years our junior, was single and, as best we could tell from his accounting of his time in college, had the luxury we had not, which was parents with plenty of money to pay for it. We would not hold this against him. Nor did it count in his favor. We had a brief evening visit to decide if we would consider having our first tenant assuming he was offered the job. I pointed to our new corner-less rug and said, "While we have pets, we are not keen on having any next door. After all, we do own the place so if something is ruined its our own fault. You're not coming with a pack of Great Danes to kennel in the backyard and two or three house cats to climb the curtains are you?" I added the extreme versions of cats and dogs so as to not come off too seriously.

"No, no critters large, small or in between. Just me and my Yamaha upright piano."

Miles said, "That you can play as loudly as you want. The walls are well sound proofed."

They got into a conversation on programming that was just too exciting for me. I sat and sipped my drink and without inquiry made another round assuming I'd have two additional takers. I did. I silently exchanged one glass for the other and resumed my seat on the couch having yielded my normal chair by the fireplace to our guest. The conversation finally shifted from work talk to play.

"I've been coming up here since my childhood," Robert said. "Every winter we went skiing up on Beech and our family would

49

rent a chalet most summers as well. It is so beautiful in the mountains."

"We certainly agree with that though neither of us ski," I pointed out. "I might as well get a little nosy. Are you dating, engaged, married, divorced? You know, any of those things the university is dying to know and can't ask. Strictly held here. Miles can leave if you wish so as to not cross-contaminate the interview process."

Robert smiled and said, "None of the above at the moment! My last roommate moved to Florida and let me know by leaving a note on the kitchen table."

We both noticed the deliberate air quotes he used when pronouncing the word roommate. By now we were far enough into the evening it seemed like some conversation was needed to either wind things up or invite him to dinner, either here or going out somewhere. I asked, "Would you be able to join us for dinner this evening?"

He didn't hesitate, "Sure!"

If I was cooking here I had to nail down the next thing. "Do you eat meat?"

"I eat everything."

"Don't look it," I said. "Well, then I will excuse myself to the kitchen and get crackin' on some vittles. I think I still have some leftover possum stew in the fridge. You did say you eat everything." I could tell he was hoping this was another Great Dane and cat exaggeration but wasn't certain. I fired up the grill and started on a salad. Opened a bottle of red wine and set the dining room table. When the grill was hot I threw on three prime rib eyes. Lucky for him the only package in the store earlier that day was a three pack. I was preparing to freeze the third but hadn't yet. It wasn't long until I called, "Dinner."

Later that week, Miles knew before Robert that the job was his should he accept. HR was instructed to extend the offer and Robert accepted. Once HR confirmed, Miles rang Robert's number and asked simply, "Do August and I have a new neighbor?"

"If you think August will give me key, then you do," adding, "I sure hope he will."

Miles put him at ease. "He's the one that went and duplicated keys the next morning." He said, 'We get any pickier than Robert and that thing will sit empty until be both croak.'"

Robert arrived with a huge U-Haul pulling his Subaru behind it. I had no idea how he loaded it, but I had a pretty good idea of how it was going to get unloaded. Still I had to play my mischievous self. "Do you have help coming over to unload?"

He had it worked out at least as a back-up plan. "My dad's coming over from Charlotte tomorrow to help with whatever I couldn't do myself."

The windows to our apartment were open. I hollered, "Miles! Git your lifitin' shoes on!" With that, we got to unloading the truck with its house full of furniture. "Where did you get all this? It's nice stuff."

He said, "I was the only one that wanted my grandma's things when she died. Their loss—my gain."

"I'll say," Miles concurred.

When we were done there was only one thing left to do. I looked at the tired lot of us and said, "Martinis?"

Chapter Nine

Robert would be a good neighbor and a good employee. Miles really enjoyed working with him, and they had a little trio from the team, Miles, Robert and Madi, who went to lunch almost every day of the work week. Once in a blue moon I would join them, but the three were obsessed with the job and talked nothing but shop. I would from time to time tell them what sewer or rat problem we were dealing with at the physical plant just to remind them that, whatever frustrations they might have with their least favorite office, at least they weren't dealing with the stench of dead rats and backed-up shit. As was my nature, I tended to exaggerate it and my role in dealing with it, as this old farm boy could talk about anything and still eat. With their sensibilities, you could see my stories almost made them ready to throw-up when I'd get into "the exploding sewer pipe that shot-up over Bobby and almost got me." There was never any exploding sewer pipe, but it was a reality that he and his crew and me, if needed, got boots and hands filthy plenty of times. I was not one of those managers who would stand idly by when it was obvious one more pair of hands was needed.

As for Robert's love life, if he had one, it would remain as much mystery and actually more so than the first night we shared martinis and rib eyes. At work, not too surprisingly, the young, single, good-looking man played it straight as an arrow. With us it was all innuendo but never coming out and just saying one way or the other. Maybe he was bi. It wouldn't have mattered to us one way or the other. We both just wanted to see him make a life with someone. I would, from time to time, even suggest he was missing out on sharing his life by saying things to Miles like, "Do you remember our one trip to Dallas when we sprung for a junior suite at the Adolphus, ate dinner in the French Room with that fantastic waiter Raul, and then had port and cigars in the lounge?" Well, of course Miles remembered it. It was the gold standard to date for our self-splurges. This was just to get us reminiscing on what was one of the most wonderful weekends of our years together. Any dog story would get us going as well. I even told Robert, "Now if you ever decide to settle down, we might even concede for you and yours to have dog or two next door so long as it a suitable breed.

No pit bulls. No Great Danes. No little yappers. Landlord review and approval required."

He would from time to time have overnight guests, but rarely just one. Maybe he was kinkier than we thought, or maybe he just wasn't inclined to any real intimacy. We kept our boundaries respectful. After ten years of living next door, he was still a bachelor. As things happened next, it was a blessing of a kind.

Robert used his vacation leave one day at a time in the winter months to go over to Beech to ski mid-week when the slopes were not as crowded. He was there from the opening to the closing every season. He had never been skiing anywhere but the North Carolina mountains. He tried Sugartop but definitely was a Beech Mountain regular. He had always wanted to go to Aspen, so one year he skipped the opening season and headed to Aspen after New Years to spend two weeks on the Colorado slopes. I may be mischievous when afforded the opportunity, but one thing I never do is make some kind of joke around accidents or death. I wish Robert had followed my rule on this.

As he was loading up to leave he said to Miles and me, "These slopes will make Beech look like a bunny-run. Let's hope I don't do a Sonny Bono."

I *hate* when people say things like that. We said in unison, "Please don't!"

He did. Just three days after he'd arrived into his two-week dream vacation we got a call from his father. Miles took the call. Robert had taken a bad spill on the slopes and was in a coma. "Things did not look good." His parents would fly out to be there. Miles had been promoted to director of administrative applications three years earlier and so technically was now Robert's boss. Robert's father asked if he needed to notify anyone else at the university. Miles assured him nothing was needed there. He would make everyone aware.

By the time they got to the hospital in Colorado, the doctors sat them down for the hard truth. There was no brain activity. A ventilator and feeding tube were keeping him alive. The doctor saw "no hope of recovery." The next morning they resigned themselves to what needed done. He was disconnected from the artificial life support and died a few minutes later—his mother and father standing at the foot of the bed. A few hours later an older sister we'd never met called to let us know.

Our friends at the Daisy Cafe knew Robert as well. He had joined us many times for breakfast over the years. We broke the news to them, and said we'd be boarding the dogs and going to Charlotte to be at the funeral home and attend the funeral. Ethel offered to stay at the apartment and take care of Jem and Scout. Jem was no longer chewing corners off the rugs. At their age they were no trouble. They had their own dog door into the backyard, and her offer to save us from having to board them was quickly and very gratefully received. We gave Ethel Miles' key, explained where their food was and their typical eating habits, which bed we would have made up if she decided to stay overnight which we left up to her—hoping she would—and we went home to pack.

We checked into a hotel in Charlotte not too far from the funeral home and waited until the next day to go over. It was a closed casket. Perhaps because of the head injury or perhaps because they just wanted it that way. We didn't ask, and they didn't say. We went around the room looking at the flowers that had arrived. The large spring mix we had ordered was there and just a bit further down was another large arrangement simply marked as from the Daisy Cafe. We finally met all three of his siblings and reintroduced ourselves to his parents who we had seen in Boone a time or two but didn't want to presume they remembered us, though knowing they surely should. Miles is a master of mourning with those who mourn. I stood back a bit in my usual more-distant self as I observed others coming and going, and observed my own grief for this fine man whose life was cut too short.

I didn't inquire about their church status. All we knew was the funeral would be in the funeral home chapel and that the older sister who called us would be leading it. She did an unremarkable job, and it was certainly more impersonal than we expected. Some family friend sang some equally unremarkable contemporary Christian song that was in tune, which was the best I could say for it. There was a good showing from the university of people in Miles' department, as well as a few others on campus who Robert had worked with. Miles was really glad to see them all there, and when Madi came in, he invited her to sit with us.

It wasn't the oddest funeral I'd ever been to but it was runner-up. When one of my employee's father died, I thought I should probably go to the funeral. I had no compunction to go the funeral home. I did let a couple of the guys he worked with know I was going if either wanted to take off work and go with me. One said he would. We arrived at a near-empty Catholic church. When the service started, the few family members present came in and sat in the front pew. They all fit in one pew on one side. I thought for a man who died in his early seventies, one would expect a lot more family, friends and neighbors. There was no music in the service, and if the priest ever met the man you couldn't tell it from his brief homily. He proceeded to deliver the most perfunctory mass any ecclesiastic mechanic could possibly perform. The family was led out by the funeral home ushers, stood in a receiving line at the door, and our fellow worker genuinely thanked us for coming, saying it meant a lot. I suspect it did.

The car doors had barely closed when my companion said, "Good god! Was it just me, or was that the most depressing funeral ever?"

I said simply, "It wasn't just you. Pitiful." Then I added, "At least we can be glad he's being buried in Tennessee, and we don't have to go to that."

He responded, "You got that right."

Robert's was now the runner-up. We did go to the graveside, which consisted of a poorly chosen poem and an equally poorly composed prayer—and that was it. When we got in the car, neither one of us could say anything for a long time. Miles spoke first, "From funeral home to grave it appeared to me that bunch had no idea who Robert was. Ethel and Maggie could have done better than that lot. And you, and me and Madi could have given him the send-off he deserved."

I had my own take adding, "I never thought he was estranged from his family, but I must say he has a strange family. Icebergs give off more warmth than that bunch. I can begin to see why he stayed single so long. He might have learned some limited degree of social politeness from the family, but there is no way he learned anything about intimacy."

We both remained mostly silent on the drive home. Ethel was just getting back to the apartment from her shift, and we went in together to two dogs who greeted us like we'd just gotten back from an extended trip to Switzerland. Tails were wagging and heads bobbing. We petted them as we told Ethel about the last couple days.

All she could say was, "How strange. I guess he got that big smile and laugh of his in spite of them."

I waited a few days to see if I would hear from one of his parents about all his things next door. When I didn't, I finally called them. His mother answered, and when I said who it was she quickly passed me off to her husband.

I started the conversation. "There is certainly no need to do anything quickly, but I did want to coordinate arrangements for Robert's furniture and personal items. Do you know when and how you'd like to handle this?"

There was a peculiarly long silence, it seemed to me, given this had to have crossed his mind before now. Was he actually too choked up to respond? Maybe they were human after all.

Maybe not. "We don't want his things. You can call a thrift store to come pick everything up if you want or sell it. Makes no difference to us."

I said, "I'm sure he must have some personal things—photos and such. What should we do with those?"

Coldly, he said, "As with the other things, it makes no difference to us."

Miles was standing there but could only hear my half of the conversation. I concluded the call by saying, "I believe you have our phone number if you change your mind on anything. As I said, we're in no rush to rent next door." He didn't say anything; he just hung up the phone. We never heard another word from him or anyone else in the family.

We felt odd "inheriting" all his furniture, but we also weren't going to just have it hauled off as some hand-me-down. We made our own valuation of the contents and donated that amount to a scholarship fund at the university in his name. Normally, we would have done such a thing anonymously. However, in this case we made sure our names were publicly acknowledged for the sole reason of his parents being able to see such was done in his memory should their disregard ever turn into regret and they found out we kept all his belongings. To our knowledge they never faced regret or knew there was a generous gift in the name of Robert Stiles.

We did one other thing to honor our friend. Madi, Ethel, Maggie, Noel, Miles and I donated a large oak tree and two park benches to the campus with simple memorial plaques to go with each. They read, "In Memory of Our Friend, Robert Jeremy Stiles, 1962 - 1997."

Robert's death was a unique kind of grief made worse by the family that made it worse. Neither of us could imagine moving in anyone next door any time soon. It would be almost two years before we even imagined the possibility. The rector of our parish said that the bishop wanted to place a curate to work with him as soon as she was ordained. The ordination was still a couple months out, but he wanted to coordinate her placement now. She was a year out of seminary and had been ordained a deacon a year earlier in Charlotte. I was treasurer by then and was consulted by the rector on the feasibility of all this. I laid out what I thought was workable and what the vestry would likely agree to. I also included an amount we would ask if she wanted to live in our apartment which was certainly within any reasonable housing allowance. He passed all this onto the bishop who talked with the curate. The vestry met and approved the plan, and arrangements were made for her to come to a Sunday service and preach as well as meet with the vestry and see the apartment later that afternoon.

And so it was that Christina became the curate and second occupant of the apartment. She was thrilled with the place and glad to have something furnished because, as she put, she was "traveling light these days." In fact she was still living with her parents. Of course, she also passed the no Great Dane pack and climbing cats test before she was given the key. She did, in fact, soon get a house cat but sought our approval in advance.

She was a very good tenant but not one we would socialize with. There were no martini evenings not that she might not imbibe. As treasurer, I wanted to maintain a completely objective and professional, if that's the correct term, working relationship with her. Knowing what I did about church politics, anything else seemed rather foolish. Finances or disagreeable circumstances might mean sacking her at some point, and I didn't need to make that any more difficult than it would already be.

Time passed. No sacking required. She left a little over five years later when she was given her first parish in the Diocese of Dallas. Some little church in another university town—Denton— that, unlike some parishes was fine having a woman rector.

Rectories were falling out of fashion but she was still packing light and was glad that they had a semi-furnished rectory she could call home. We heard from her each year at Christmas with the usual "mail to everyone you know" Christmas letter. We enjoyed hearing her story as it progressed. She married a Denton man, they added two children to their family over the course of the years, and the little Denton parish seemed to appreciate her enough to give her job security as long as she wanted. As the years passed, it seemed that would be a long time.

We had a series of unremarkable young faculty who rented from us for one or two academic years after Christina left. They came and went, and we never got attached to any of them. In some cases I would have to dig out my records to even recall their names. I suppose that's a bit exaggerated but not by much. We grew tired of the turnover and the degree of deep cleaning each move-out required. Clearly a couple of them didn't know what a dust rag was or how to clean a shower. Thank goodness we held the line on pets. I'm sure the way some of them came and left, they would have had destructive, psychotic animals out of sheer neglect.

Finally, fed up with the new faculty route and no curate in sight any time soon, we just left the apartment empty with the notion that the spirit would have to move us before we gave anyone else the key.

Silence. I gave him a minute to come out of whatever dream state he must be in. I still didn't hear anything. I went in to look. The body neither warm nor cold. Eyes open, staring up at the ceiling. No life in them.

Each morning before getting up he would say the Rosary. There it was in his hand, across his chest, on a bead about half way through. The Rosary was his practice not mine, but I found myself saying out loud over the lifeless body, "Holy Mary, mother of God, pray for us sinners now and at the hour of our death. Amen."

I gently took the rosary from his stiffening hand, and closed his eyes. Then the oddest thing popped into my mind. I recalled the last line of Frost's poem, *Death of the Hired Man*. I walked back to the living room where Penny-girl had curled up by my chair. I said out loud to her as though she had sent me in to check as Frost's Mary had done with Warren, "'Dead,' was all he said."

It was confirmed. His heart quit. Nothing more spectacular than that. Apparently, weaker than he or his doctors knew. The way we would all go if we could. I know for a fact he wasn't thinking his time was up just yet, but he made two things clear over our years together. He was not to live longer than me, and I was to live alone the rest of my life once he was gone. That had been the rules as set forth by him from our first year together way back in Anderson. As the years passed, it certainly was more likely the second half of that demand would indeed be respected. The only thing I ever wondered about in that arrangement was who would ever find me dead? It might be months or years before anyone noticed. As long as I was still walking up to the Daisy Cafe I assumed they would notice, and Ethel with her key would come and check to see if I'd given up the ghost or was lying helpless in a heap.

Now here was this heap lying on his bed. I took Penny-girl in to see that he was gone. I'd always made sure the living dog saw the departed sibling as I believe they know and need to see to understand they were not abandoned. I've heard cats have some sense of the death as soon as it happens and sometimes jump around the room. If dogs have that immediate sense, I'd never spotted it. She looked, I lifted her old frame from the bed and back down to the floor, and we both left the room. I sat in my chair for a while. Ethel and Maggie will be wondering where we are. Should I call them? How many people call a restaurant first? I thought I should probably call 911 first but chose not to. I wasn't that eager to see him hauled off to the morgue.

Maggie answered.

"Maggie, it's August. Miles passed away in the night. Very peacefully. I didn't even know that he was gone until I went in to check why he wasn't up."

Maggie had a one word response, "Shit!"

"I'll let you know more when I know more. Thanks, Maggie." And I hung up the phone.

The ambulance and Ethel arrived at the same time. We both stood in the living room as the two paramedics confirmed he was too long dead for them to do anything. That fact was so obvious, I guess they just thought they needed to say it to sound compassionate. Then they returned to the bedroom, put him on the gurney and would let the coroner decide if there was any foul play —a fact I knew but not one they stated. Since the police were never called, they clearly didn't suspect anything other than another old man not seeing another day. In truth, while we called ourselves old men ever since we retired, neither of us was really old by standards these days, but we would be foolish at this age to pretend death was some distant unimaginable thing. It was now reality.

As they brought him out of the bedroom, they stopped to give me a phone number to call when I was ready to have the funeral home coordinate picking up the body from the coroner. From the porch, Ethel and I watched as he was wheeled down the sidewalk and loaded into the ambulance. The ambulance began to pull away. Lights on. No siren. A neighbor across the street we didn't know well was outside looking on. With a deep sigh and just staring at nothing in particular I said, "As Margaret Houlihan said in a *M*A*S*H* episode, 'It never ceases to amaze me. One minute you are alive and the next you're dead.'"

Somehow, between our experience with Robert's funeral and our long absence from our church where we were technically still members, (though by canon law not members in good standing), we both had decided cremation, no service and ashes interred in the dog cemetery. He was not going into the Bayou Teche. On the following Monday when the cafe was closed Madi, Ethel, Maggie and Noel came over to the house for a potluck lunch. Penny-girl gave her two barks invoking her displeasure upon their arrival and retreated to the bedroom. Before we ate, we proceeded into the backyard. We went back to where I had dug a small hole before their arrival. I put the ashes in, laid his rosary gently onto the ash heap and filled hole again. I had given each a card with these words which we then recited together. The lapsed and active Catholics, Noel and Madi, would know them well. The two protestants who had joined us would utter a prayer they'd never likely thought they would, but did that day.

Hail Mary, full of grace. The Lord is with thee. Blessed art thou amongst women and blessed is the fruit of thy womb, Jesus. Holy Mary, mother of God, pray for us sinners now and at the hour of our death. Amen.

Knowing I could not, Madi at my request read *Eddi's Service.*

Eddi, priest of St. Wilfrid
 In his chapel at Manhood End,
Ordered a midnight service
 For such as cared to attend.

But the Saxons were keeping Christmas,
 And the night was stormy as well.
Nobody came to service,
 Though Eddi rang the bell.

"'Wicked weather for walking,"
 Said Eddi of Manhood End.
"But I must go on with the service
 For such as care to attend."

The altar-lamps were lighted, --
 An old marsh-donkey came,
Bold as a guest invited,
 And stared at the guttering flame.

The storm beat on at the windows,
 The water splashed on the floor,
And a wet, yoke-weary bullock
 Pushed in through the open door.

"How do I know what is greatest,
 How do I know what is least?
That is My Father's business,"
 Said Eddi, Wilfrid's priest.

"But -- three are gathered together --
 Listen to me and attend.
I bring good news, my brethren!"
 Said Eddi of Manhood End.

And he told the Ox of a Manger
 And a Stall in Bethlehem,
And he spoke to the Ass of a Rider,
 That rode to Jerusalem.

They steamed and dripped in the chancel,
 They listened and never stirred,
While, just as though they were Bishops,
 Eddi preached them The Word,

Till the gale blew off on the marshes
 And the windows showed the day,
And the Ox and the Ass together
 Wheeled and clattered away.

And when the Saxons mocked him,
 Said Eddi of Manhood End,
"I dare not shut His chapel
 On such as care to attend."

It wasn't Miles, but she did real good. It didn't seem to me anything else was needed. That poem will always take me to tears and joy for our life together—*we dare not shut His chapel on such as care to attend.*

Now the only thing to be decided was how to mark the spot where the cremains of a life and the rosary had been returned to the earth. Each dog had a simple pet stone with their name and years of life. Perhaps I would do the same for Miles, and the next owners would wonder if this was the spot of the oldest living dog in history. Or should I upgrade to a proper granite marker of some modest size. I had always kidded Miles that I knew if I betrayed his request and died first, I would surely be lucky to get even one of the pet stones. Below the single paw print it would read, "August - 1956 -?" I ordered up a flat stone just large enough to include his full name and the years—Miles Francois Bergeron, 1956-2011. Hopefully, when my time comes I'll have some friend who will complete the family burial plot in the back corner of our beloved homestead before the executor sells it off to the next owner. The law firm that is the designated executor has my instructions for the "disposition of cremains," though I'd rather it be done by a friend. I suppose that will depend on how old and decrepit I get before giving up my last breath. So far, the years were coming on faster than my decrepit state. It could be a while, unless I'm lucky enough to go as Miles had gone before me. I was certain to honor the second part of his request. I would live alone the rest of my life and be happy to do so.

Part III

Family of Pappy & Momma Daisy Jemison

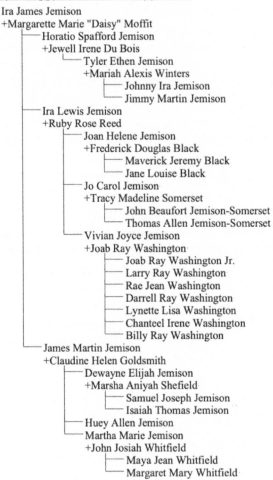

Ira James Jemison
+Margarette Marie "Daisy" Moffit
    ├── Horatio Spafford Jemison
    +Jewell Irene Du Bois
        └── Tyler Ethen Jemison
        +Mariah Alexis Winters
            ├── Johnny Ira Jemison
            └── Jimmy Martin Jemison
    ├── Ira Lewis Jemison
    +Ruby Rose Reed
        ├── Joan Helene Jemison
        +Frederick Douglas Black
            ├── Maverick Jeremy Black
            └── Jane Louise Black
        ├── Jo Carol Jemison
        +Tracy Madeline Somerset
            ├── John Beaufort Jemison-Somerset
            └── Thomas Allen Jemison-Somerset
        └── Vivian Joyce Jemison
        +Joab Ray Washington
            ├── Joab Ray Washington Jr.
            ├── Larry Ray Washington
            ├── Rae Jean Washington
            ├── Darrell Ray Washington
            ├── Lynette Lisa Washington
            ├── Chanteel Irene Washington
            └── Billy Ray Washington
    └── James Martin Jemison
    +Claudine Helen Goldsmith
        ├── Dewayne Elijah Jemison
        +Marsha Aniyah Shefield
            ├── Samuel Joseph Jemison
            └── Isaiah Thomas Jemison
        ├── Huey Allen Jemison
        └── Martha Marie Jemison
        +John Josiah Whitfield
            ├── Maya Jean Whitfield
            └── Margaret Mary Whitfield

Chapter Eleven

The Jemisons of Macon, Georgia were a formidable force. They were in many ways the best a family can imagine itself to be, but they also possessed the misfits that caused concern and grief, and they carried more than their share of tragedy. Regardless, the matriarch and patriarch of the family were solid rocks and guiding lights that would guide Tyler throughout his life.

Momma Daisy's favorite hymn was *It Is Well with My Soul*. And she knew the story behind the hymn—how Horatio Spafford's four daughters had perished when a French steamer went down in the sea. Later, when he passed over their watery graves, he was moved to pen the words of that hymn.

She'd say, "You know it's the good Lord bubblin' up in you when you stare headlong into your own grief and find words like that."

Momma and Pappy were a sight. Here was this big woman next to a rail-thin man six inches shorter than she and about as big around as one of her legs. She always said she did all she could to fatten him up, but it never took. They'd known each other since Sunday school and both graduated high school together, which wasn't too common in those days. Right after she graduated she said, "I do" to Ira James Jemison and as she put it, "Never looked back."

When her first boy came along, she named him Horatio Spafford Jemison. Pappy always took everything in stride. He knew suggesting that the first born be named after him was a waste of time.

He said once to Tyler, "I knew I was gonna have to write a powerful hymn to ever get her to name anything after me." But that wasn't all together true. The next boy she named Ira and the one after that was James.

Tyler's boy Jimmy was named after his Uncle James. He thought about naming his first son after Ira, but Uncle Ira stopped it saying, "Ain't no boy these days wants an ole-fashion name like that. And don't you think about calling your boy Horatio. That's even worse. Your daddy was a good man but I don't think he wanted a long line of Horatio Spafford Jemisons. You should call him Johnny, cause Johnny shoulda come marching home and never did git to."

Tyler was told Momma always called her first-born Horatio. Everybody else thought that was big a name for a little boy, and the nickname Hory stuck. Uncle Ira told Tyler, "The only other person I know that never would use the nickname was your daddy. It humored your Pappy to hear this little boy introduce himself to strangers as Horatio Spafford Jemison as though to cull it down would make him less than he was—less than his Momma Daisy would want of him."

Uncle Ira was right; he shoulda come marching home and never did. You see, July Fourth was no holiday in the Jemison family. It was instead a time of remembrance and sorrow. It's hard to see how the 4th would be a celebration for any descendant of slaves, but it was purely recent and personal for Momma Daisy and Pappy.

When Tyler's daddy graduated high school, he left Macon to work in Atlanta, planning to work some and go to college. When he started taking classes, he met Tyler's Momma, Jewell Irene Du Bois. Her father was, for a black man in those days, a well-to-do lawyer— funny how lighter skin afforded even the black man an open door here and there that the darker brothers found sealed tight. Tyler's daddy was definitely of the dark skin persuasion just like his momma, and Mr. Du Bois didn't like Horatio from the start. Tyler's daddy, out of love, and his mother, Jewell Irene, perhaps a bit out of spite to her father, eloped and quickly Jewell was pregnant with Tyler. But the nation had other ideas for the newlyweds. No sooner did his dad know he was going to have a child than the government called him up in the draft. It wasn't long until he was out of boot camp and on his way to Vietnam.

Up until then, both Momma and Pappy would have said you need to step-up when you're called to do so. In this war, neither could understand what "those poor people in their rice paddies had to do with poor black people in Georgia." It seemed to Momma, in particular, that they had more in common with them than the people doling out the orders. Tyler's mother came to stay with Momma and Pappy when his daddy shipped out. And she would stay there through his birth. You might say Momma Daisy was the first person to greet Tyler in this world. She was midwife and caretaker.

Tyler was only two weeks old when the telegram arrived. Private Horatio Spafford Jemison. Killed in action. July 4, 1971. It's doubtful the private ever saw the letter from Momma with Tyler's infant picture. They'd never see his body. He'd been blown to bits. They learned years later, by "friendly fire." Eventually, one of his dog tags came back to them along with a hand-delivered medal and flag. By then, Jewell had gone back to Atlanta to stay with her folks and left Tyler, for some time away it was understood, with Momma and Pappy. Momma answered the door when the soldier arrived. She had enough heart to thank him since it wasn't his fault he had such a task to perform. But she didn't invite him in either. She took the dog tag and put it in the hall bureau. The flag and medal she set on the kitchen table.

Pappy told Tyler the rest of the story when he was twenty-one. Up until then, he didn't know there was a flag or a medal.

Momma told Pappy, "Come nightfall, we're going into the chicken run and diggin' two holes. One for that flag and one for that metal."

"Pappy was perplexed by this and asked, "Why at night, why bury 'em, why in two holes and why in the chicken run?"

As Pappy told it, she had it all worked out. The buryin' was easy. She never wanted to see either one again, and they'd do it at night for the darkness the war had brought. The two holes—one for the hole their son's death left in their life and the other for the hole it would leave in the boy's. And to her the chicken run was the most obvious of all.

"I want them chickens shitting on that flag and that medal just like that president and his generals shit on us! At least somethin' good come out of chicken shit. Nothin' *ever* good come out'a war!"

Pappy told Tyler that was the only time he ever heard Momma use the word *shit* and the closest she ever came to cursin' another human being.

Momma saved the dog tag to put under a headstone at the old pond cemetery. She sent a letter to Tyler's mother to tell her when the headstone was coming so she could come home then and be there with the rest of the family when they said their last goodbye.

Momma and Pappy hadn't heard from her since she'd left for Atlanta. A couple days later, a letter arrived from her mother. It just said that Jewell had died of an overdose, and since they had the boy it seemed best they leave things as they were. Mrs. Du Bois said they would put money aside if the boy ever wanted to go to college, but beyond that they didn't want to "make any further claim" on Tyler. Until that talk with Pappy, it had all been a mystery to Tyler. They had told him his mother was dead—had died in Atlanta, but they never said how and didn't seem to want to tell him. All Momma ever said about his other grandparents was they had a haughty spirit and didn't deserve a boy like him.

They were right to wait, of course. Even feeding that in little bites to a boy would have been a lot to weigh him down. Knowing his daddy died in the war and his mother was dead was weight enough. Tyler was just glad when he turned twenty-one that Pappy laid out the whole of it—good, bad and in between. He supposed the Du Bois would have made good their promise to pay for his college, but he never tried to find out. Nor did they come looking for him. Momma and Pappy didn't want their money, and even though when Tyler learned the story, he still could have made a claim, he didn't want it either.

Up until that night burial in the chicken yard, Tyler's Uncle James told him Pappy had a flag hanging from the porch every holiday there was. He had little flags up and down the sidewalk on the 4th. He'd served as a Navy cook in World War II under a southern white chief who didn't consider himself a bigot but was one true enough. Still, Pappy felt loyalty to the service and would even hang the flag out on Christmas Eve. Momma didn't think the baby Jesus needed that flag flying on his behalf, but she let him hang it out there with the Christmas lights. That night in the chicken yard was the end of his flag flying. Tyler didn't know what he did with them, but they were never in Momma's house again— he knew that. And he didn't think Pappy minded one bit. Vietnam turned his mind from what duty to country meant, and he was to never turn back again.

Every 4th, when the fire works started, Momma would stand on the porch lookin' towards the park and say loud enough for anyone within earshot to hear loud and clear, "The rich men of this country ain't got no right to send poor boys off to die for their sins." And with those words off that big chest, she'd go back in, sit still in her rocker and read the twenty-second Psalm. She'd read it aloud— reading right through the explosions going on down the street. Between the booms you could hear her from the porch. When she was done with it, she'd sit with the Bible in her lap until the fireworks were over. And when the quiet came back to the place, she would start rocking in her chair and would sing softly to herself and her dead boy that hymn—*It Is Well with My Soul*. And the young Tyler knew it was the good Lord bubblin' up in her when she could stare headlong into her own grief and sing like an angel.

Momma always liked for Tyler to know who was connected to whom and how. Her methodology in laying this out was always the same. She'd start from the most recent and work her way back. This amused Tyler's boys because if someone's name came up and they were dead the account would begin with, "That'n dead." Then they'd hear how they died, who came to the funeral, what songs were sung, what the minister said, where they were buried and what food they had afterward. Then she had a list of who didn't come to the funeral and should have. Only then would connections begin to be laid out in detail along with children, marriages, divorces and any "movin' from place to place" that had gone on. A high school friend of Tyler's was at the house for Easter dinner once, and ran into one of her longer discourses when he asked how she knew his grandma.

He said to Tyler afterwards, "If I ask my mom about someone she just says, 'Oh, that's a cousin of mine.' That's it."

Tyler laughed at such a thin answer, "Momma lays it out the same way she lays out Easter dinner. You're gonna get a feast and never leave hungry."

I told Tyler my mother was somewhere in between. She came from a big family, as most Mennonite families were back in those days. It seemed like everywhere we went there was a cousin, great aunt, great uncle—directly or by marriage. She seemed to operate with a crystal-clear family tree in her head including the children born down to the present time. This was a gift she did not pass on to her children. I was the one most interested in the ancestors, but working my way forward comes to a quick dead end. I can name all my nieces and nephews, but if I even tried to call up half their offspring I'd come up short. As for my cousins kids'—forget it! I don't have a clue.

Chapter Twelve

Momma Daisy and Pappy had three children. It seemed possible that they might have wanted more given Momma's love of children, but if they did they never said. Neither were of the kind to lament the could-ha-beens of life or even the should-da-beens. They took each day with gratitude for what was and certainly passed on the importance of that to their three boys.

Ira Lewis was two years younger than Tyler's dad and James Martin three years younger than he. As a boy, Ira loved anything of wood and would tinker in the garage with Pappy's tools. In high school, he took industrial arts and that's where he made Momma Daisy's rocker for his senior project. The gymnasium was filled with youngsters' handiwork. Third place went to a boy who'd taken various and sundry old pieces of wood his dad had salvaged for some future possibility, and the boy turned them into a handsome dining room table. Another built a pecan-cased grandfather clock. Both these boys gave Ira tough competition. But there really was no contest when you looked closely at that rocking chair. It was exquisite.

Mr. Huber, the industrial arts teacher, told Pappy, "I could never have done that fine of work if I took a year to do it."

A lot of people from the community came to the fair. Many of the boys and the one girl in the class had prices on their work if anyone was interested in buying them. Ira's project had a sign taped to the floor in front of the chair which simply read, "Not for Sale." When Momma Daisy and Pappy went through the show, Ira was insistent that she sit in it to see if it fit as good as he'd hoped it would. She sat down as gently as the big woman could, put her hands on each arm, head back and started to gently rock. Ira wondered if she was gonna start singing a hymn. It wouldn't have surprised him. Instead, she rocked a minute or two and said simply with a big grin, "It don't even need no breakin' in." She got up and caressed the top of it a few times and gave Ira one of her great Momma bear hugs whispering in his ear, "You done real good, Ira-boy. Real good."

The one girl in the class was Ruby Rose Reed. Ira couldn't decide if he liked this girl for the rhythm of her name, the ordered construction of each name with its four letters—as he did like order, or the fact that she was brave enough to take a class that up till then was always only boys, or if pretty looks and a strong demeanor suggested he might be just a little bit in love with Ruby Rose Reed. She had crafted a stained glass window in the prairie style, and Ira was convinced that the all-male judging team passed by her work too quickly when they saw a young girl standing next to it as its creator. He was probably right. Even Ira thought all the labor of the chair probably deserved first place, but he was fairly persuaded that the clock and table should have been downgraded one notch to give Ruby Rose Reed's window second spot.

When Momma Daisy was up and out of the chair, Ira walked Momma and Pappy down the aisle to show them the window. He also introduced them to her saying, "Here's the finest young woman in the school, miss Ruby Rose Reed. She's Methodist but she's a real good person, and her daddy is the minister and her momma the organist. As you can see, an artist as well as a craftsman...or is it craftswoman? Anyway, Ruby this is Momma Daisy and my daddy, Ira James."

Ruby surprised all of them when she reached out, shook both their hands with the strength of a man and said, "And one day I might be a Jemison if this lug-head would see I'm crazy about him. Why did he think I got in this class in the first place?"

Pappy was both amused and impressed by her and looked at Ira, "Boy, I think this young lady just proposed to you. You might wanna think about doing something about that."

Ira was never one to be embarrassed easily, but he was noticeably knocked off his guard by this unexpected exchange. Momma Daisy could see it and thought she might as well add her own two cents. "Ira Lewis, I had to do the same thing with that lug-head you call your daddy. Jemison men are slow to see when a good woman is in love with them."

Ruby Rose Reed could hardly contain herself. As she'd done with Momma Daisy and Ira James, she reached out to shake Ira's hand, gripping it and shaking it the whole time she talked. "Ira Jemison, should you decide to court me for a time, I'm ready when you are. Should you decide to marry me, well, with your woodwork and my windows we could make a beautiful home."

They didn't court long. Three weeks after the industrial arts show they both graduated high school, three weeks after that they announced their engagement, three weeks after that they were married, and three weeks after that they'd bought their first and what would be their last house.

It was only a house then. No one had cared for it in years—if ever. It was continually rented out to people who by nature always left something worse than they found it. It was getting so run-down that the lazy, old owner was tired dealing with it and certainly wasn't going to put any money into fixing it up. Ira and Ruby were both eager to buy the cheapest and ugliest house in the neighborhood, as they wanted to transform it into "as pretty a house as anywhere in town." Ruby's parents had given her "a nest egg to start a family" and Momma Daisy and Ira James had done the same. They took the two nest eggs, paid cash for "the dump" as Momma Daisy had long referred to the house, and they set out to make it a home.

The industrial arts teacher made his contractor connections well aware of the skills Ira had. Without looking, he had plenty of jobs doing finish work in new homes and some heftier remodel projects. He was getting regular work from three different contractors, and each appreciated his skills to the point that if they had to wait for him to juggle jobs, they managed to convince most home owners to be patient—that they wouldn't be disappointed if they waited for Ira. There would be those that want everything yesterday that wouldn't wait and then the contractors' general attitude in bringing in someone else was "suit yourself."

Realtors walking into some of the finer homes in Macon could spot his work in an instant. They would be sure to tell clients, "All the woodwork in this house is the craftsmanship of Ira Jemison." They said it as though if you didn't know who Ira Jemison was, you should. Ira was always pleased when given the opportunity to work at least one of Ruby's windows into a job as well which the realtors also admired. They would add, "And these fine leaded windows are the work of Ruby Jemison, Ira's wife."

Both Ira and Ruby were never rushed to see how quickly something could be done, but neither were they dawdlers. They would be certain to do some work every evening and weekends on their own house. The only vacation time they seemed to ever want was making "the dump" something fresh and new. Ruby scraped off every inch of layered paint that covered what Ira was sure would be cypress clapboards. He had a very specific earth-tone color palette in mind for the exterior and wanted to transform the shabby, white frame house into a Craftsman gem. He would add new detail to overhangs and build a new front porch. They worked into their design a number of prairie-style leaded, stained glass windows and replaced all the other windows with frames Ira built and Ruby glazed. Inside they added a stone fireplace which Pappy and James built together. Ira paneled walls, built doors and cabinets, and added coffered ceilings in the now-open living and dining rooms. Ruby built three beautiful prairie-style stained glass windows for above the dining buffet that Ira would build "when the house was far enough along." Together they constructed an elegant front door of oak and stained glass.

Neither was happy with the roof on the house, but neither did they want to put just any old roof on it. In those days there were fewer options for a good metal roof. What they wanted was a weathered, standing seam, copper roof. A few of the nicest homes in Macon had such a roof and to both their minds, nothing would suit their transformed dump better. By the time the old roof had to come off, they had saved enough to put on the copper so long as they did all the work themselves. Undaunted as usual, they tackled the project. When it was done Ira said to Ruby, "It ought to see us out."

Somehow their life always seemed to flow in a natural rhythm of three. In their third year of marriage came their first child, a girl. Three years later came a second girl. Then somehow things got out of synch and neither would be too happy with the end result. The third girl, Vivian Joyce, came two years after the second, and from the start, they could see she was going to be anything but a lady. They tried all different ways of arresting the impending outcome, to no avail. In her terrible twos Ira told Ruby, "I'm going for the snip. Our luck has run out."

Ruby said, "I'll drive you there!"

Vivian Joyce Jemison went from a screaming, selfish child to a bossy, homely woman. She married a fellow of equally unpleasant disposition, Joab Washington, and together they proceeded to have one child after the other. She was only fifteen when she was pregnant with her first. Ira and Ruby came home from working together and found their youngest coming towards the front door with a small suitcase packed.

Ruby asked, "Where you going?"

She started in her usual sassy voice, "Joab and I are going off to get married. I'm gonna have his baby. We're in love, and he says he needs a real woman like me. He's real proud of what he got down there."

Ira couldn't have stopped his head from shaking if he'd tried which he did not. The ignorance and belligerence of this child of theirs would never cease to amaze them both. They had seen Joab drop Vivian off in his old Ford wagon after school and were afraid a day like this was coming. Ruby talked to her about birth control, but that clearly sailed in one ear and out the other like anything of sense always did with Vivian. The same week Vivian learned she was pregnant, Joab—who was two years older but only one grade ahead of Vivian from being held back his freshman year—had been suspended for three weeks. As Ira heard the story later, he had asked his teacher in the last section of the day to be excused to go to the restroom. There were only ten minutes left in the class, so the teacher told him to wait as he was sure Joab was just wanting to cut out early. Joab went to the back of the class and proceeded to piss in the waste basket. He had been suspended a day or two over the years but with this longer suspension, he never went back. He got a job in a tire shop where he always managed to have enough money to get his monthly *Playboy*, and would pin up the centerfold in the bay where he worked.

Theirs was a real love story from the start. Vivian took up with three other girls who would go out every day after school and smoke under the bleachers. It wasn't long before Joab and the pack he ran with from the same high school as Joab found these girls from the Macon school, and in no time Joab and Vivian skipped the bleachers and headed every day to that Ford where they would drive out in the woods and "stimulate their carnal desires" as Momma Daisy would classify such goings-on.

Ira looked at this pitiful girl and said, "Vivian, how your idea of love can be so different from what your Momma Daisy and Pappy and your momma and I have is beyond me. You'd be a lot better off worrying about what he's got between those ears and how he's using them brains. This fool notion of him being proud of, as you put it, 'what he's got down there' may be the dumbest thing I've ever heard. A man ain't got nothin' to be proud of or ashamed of when it comes to the body he was given. He had nothin' to do with it. If you try to make a life around that kind of foolishness, you're never going to know anything close to real love."

She headed out the door, "We'll just see about that!"

Ira asked Ruby, "Do we try to stop her?"

Ruby said, "She thinks she's got wings. Let her try to fly."

The two moved into an old half-dilapidated camper that sat out back at Joab's folks' place. They would rent a small mobile home and then another, as the family grew by one most every year, until they finally got a loan on a repo double-wide which they parked where the camper had been. When Vivian announced number six was on the way, Ira couldn't hold his tongue any longer. "Good god woman! Misery loves company, I guess."

At family gatherings, it was hard to decide who was the worse behaved—the parents or their children. All the Jemisons were glad their last name was Washington. As Pappy said, "Maybe with that last name, people won't connect 'em with us."

Joab was not a churchgoer and Vivian was happy enough to join him in avoiding church. Momma Daisy, who would normally be concerned for their souls, was more concerned for the Sunday school teachers. "Thank the lord those ladies who volunteer to teach the children every Sunday don't need to put up with that Washington mess." When reflecting on the poor school teachers who had the "Washington mess" five days a week she had just one thing to say, "Lord, have mercy."

Pappy's speculation was that between detention and the principal's office the teachers got some break at least. All the Jemison grandchildren and parents were glad the "Washington mess" was in a different school district. Interaction was minimal and Ira learned early on when they came hat-in-hand to send them off, "before they learned to make a habit of it," which they certainly would have done. Given the laziness and disagreeable nature of both Vivian and Joab, none of the Jemisons could ever quite figure out how they got by from one month to the next, or how one or more of them had avoided incarceration up to this point. Somehow they had. They weren't so curious as to ascertain exactly how.

All the Jemisons picked up on Momma Daisy's label as the appropriate announcement of their arrival at any function. Whoever was first to spot them pull up would warn everyone else, "The Washington mess is here."

When the mess was present, no gathering could go by without Vivian and Joab launching into a swearing match over any of the dumbest things and with the children wreaking havoc of their own. Their cousins took all efforts to steer clear. In some respects they were a wonder to behold. If there was any love in that household, it was buried out of everyone else's sight. They never divorced, never had two nickels to rub together, never improved anything for any reason, lived in that crowded double-wide outside of Macon which Momma Daisy referred to as "the dump." "Ira got rid of the dump in town only to have his daughter make a worse mess out Johnson Road. Thank the good lord, Washington is the name on that mailbox," she'd say.

There was an unwritten agreement between the Jemisons that if one or more of the Washington children did try to break free, all would be done to help the child recover. So far, none had. They all hoped that somehow out of the chaos that was the Washingtons, at least one would go off and find a better life at the first opportunity. So far of the mixed lot of hellion boys and potty-mouth girls, none appeared headed in a good direction. They seemed to be chips off the old blocks.

Ira and Ruby's other two girls were both late to marry—one to a good man and one to a good woman. That second marriage got some raised eyebrows from the church crowd even among the Methodists where Ira and Ruby attended. As was often the case, Ruby's father was moved to a new congregation so they lost their good pastor and organist in one move. Among Ruby's artistic gifts was playing organ, so they weren't without one even a Sunday. She had never played for the congregation, and her mother never needed a substitute. Like everything Ruby put her mind to, she woke them all up with her rousing introduction to that first hymn that first Sunday. The minister who was there when the second marriage was to come about wouldn't bless two women. Neither the church nor he approved of such abominations.

Overhearing the discussion at Momma Daisy and Pappy's, Johnny asked, "What's an abomination?"

Momma Daisy answered as matriarch of the family, "Johnny, that' when someone decides you're a sinner and they're not."

"That don't sound Christian to me," Johnny responded.

"Nor should it," Pappy replied.

The girls went to Massachusetts to get their license and had their ceremony in Ira and Ruby's backyard. Ira had told his girls when they were younger that he didn't mind walking them down an aisle, but they shouldn't have the minister ask, "Who gives this woman to be married?" He said, "I don't possess you. You're here on loan to your mother and me until you're ready to make your own way. I can't give away what ain't mine to give."

The two women walked down the garden path together. The gathering included all the Jemisons except the Washington mess whose invitation got lost between the kitchen table and the mailbox, and one sister from the other side of the family as they didn't approve. When Vivian found out about the wedding through the grapevine, she asked her mother about how she could support such a thing.

Ruby said, "Vivian, if you didn't see that girl didn't like boys growin' up, then you're even dumber than I thought. Momma Daisy knew it too. She said, 'God gave us that girl to open our eyes.' Maybe it's time you open yours. And when it comes to gettin' your own house in order, you got more work to do than the rest of us combined."

A good two years passed after that before Ruby ever heard another word from Vivian or saw the Washington mess. All the Jemisons appreciated the respite.

In the end, Ira and Ruby had eleven grandchildren. A girl and a boy born to their oldest daughter Joan and her husband Frederick. The second daughter, Jo Carol and her wife Tracy, fostered two twin boys from a terrible mess of a home and were able to adopt them. And Vivian finally quit at seven.

Chapter Thirteen

James was a different kind of craftsman from his brother Ira. Pappy was a stone and brick mason and up until James graduated from high school, Pappy had always worked for someone else. The pair decided to strike out on their own. Both men had far more strength than their small frames seemed to suggest. They worked well together, and with Ira's growing reputation among the finer contractors in Macon, it wasn't long before Jemison Masonry had all the work they could handle. While they would lay brick, both men preferred the artistry of stone work.

Pappy, Ira and James would themselves never live in a stone or brick home, but driving by you could spot the Jemison homes. Each had a large stone chimney, stone accents on the front porch, fine wood detail and Ruby's stained glass windows. Their three homes alone increased the property values of the entire neighborhood. Few would scrape the paint off as Ruby had setting the standard for the Jemisons, but several neighbors began showing greater care in their yards and gardens and venturing beyond white to brighten up their homes with older historical colors. It was a neighborhood of transition without the gentrification that so often drove families out. This was building from strength to strength one house at a time.

On their first job together, they laid up a stone fireplace and did a flagstone patio for a family by the name of Goldsmith. Not that it matters, but they were a mixed-race couple which wasn't all that rare by then, but the Jemison men couldn't deny noticin'. They had a sweet and pretty daughter, Claudine Helen, who would bring the crew lemonade twice a day—mid morning and mid afternoon. Tea, if any preferred, but James and Pappy stuck with the fresh-squeezed lemonade. Before long, she started bringing little sandwiches with the drinks. She always seemed to congregate near James. One afternoon when she'd finally gone back inside from where they were working on the flagstone, Pappy said to his son, "She might be sweet on you. You know your momma says we Jemison men are always the last to know. She is a pretty thing."

You could see the lightbulb go off above James's head. Such an idea pleased him very much. Next time she came out, he decided to test the waters. He didn't even know her name to that point.

"Ms. Goldsmith, might you consider going to a movie with me this Saturday?"

"You don't have to call me Ms. My name is Claudine— Claudine Helen Goldsmith. I hear your father call you James. What's your full name? I like to know the boys I go out with in case the police stop us."

"I'm James Martin Jemison who has never been stopped by the police, but who is not so naive as to discount the possibility. What about Saturday?"

She said, "Sounds charming. When would you like to pick me up?"

One might think there is much more to their story, but really it is pretty simple. That Saturday led to Sunday church together. She was Episcopalian which was a new experience for James, but he thought it was interesting. Every Saturday and every Sunday became a routine for them until they decided Monday through Friday sounded even better. That took about six months and Ira, having already bought the ugliest house in the neighborhood, left them to buy the only other rental which the same man owned and with the same careless concern. With Ira's fixed up, this second-place ugly had moved into first place.

Ira and Ruby's backyard had given way to a post and beam barn the two hand crafted that was divided in two parts—one for his workshop and the other for Ruby's. Ira was sure to seal it well between the two sections so that his sawdust didn't interfere with her windows. Both parts were illuminated in part by the natural light that came in through the windows Ruby built for each. To say it was the handsomest barn in Macon would have been an understatement. It was far more handsome than the vast majority of homes.

Instead of a barn, James and Claudine, who both loved their hands in the dirt, put in as big a garden as they could fit. They fenced it in to keep out rabbits, though they threw plenty of the harvest their way. Neither boy needed to worry about eggs. Momma Daisy's chickens thrived through some special blessing due her for losing her oldest in that war as she reckoned it, and

James and Claudine's garden seem to possess the same blessing. Whatever they put in the ground grew to prize-winning quality, quantity and proportion, though neither of them would ever enter anything in the county fair. All the produce from their garden went to feed Jemisons and half the neighborhood. They would never take any money from anyone, though they wouldn't turn down some barter for something just to return gratitude for gratitude. They particularly liked heaping produce on the Delagranges who, in turn, came each fall with a case full of their homemade mincemeat—the kind with real meat—which both of them loved.

And as the Delagranges dropped off their repayment they would add, "And the other case is for you to split with your folks and your brother."

"We're sure gonna be thankful for you on Thanksgiving day when we pass around mincemeat pies. We do thank you." James didn't worry much about creativity in his thank you. From one year to the next it was mostly the same. Sometimes Christmas. Sometimes Thanksgiving. Neither was an exaggeration as they passed around mincemeat pies on both holidays.

James and Claudine had two boys and a girl. All baptized Episcopalian as babies. Momma Daisy said, "I don't see a baby needs a priest to pour water on it to go to heaven, but I don't see how it hurts either." She herself, along with Pappy and their three boys, were all immersed when they were "old enough to make a profession," but Pappy said, "Quakers don't baptize and I figure they are as good by Lord as anybody." They were both gifted in letting their children find their own way. Both had observed parents who tried to force things their way, and as Momma Daisy said, "All you get with that is heartache and mad children." And then she would add, as though this answered any doubt about the freedom they gave their boys, "The good tree will bear fruit in due season."

Dewayne was the oldest of James and Claudine, and after a couple years in junior college, he decided to start working with his dad full-time if he'd have him. Pappy was wanting to work part-time by then so the timing was good. Dewayne was about the size of the two put together. Pappy was a little concerned about such a big fella climbing up scaffolding, but Dewayne seem to manage it just fine. And once on the scaffold, he could pick up a rock like it was made just for that spot.

Pappy was quick to say that the boy had what it took to be a fine stone mason. "Musta got it from his Pappy!" Pappy was good, but knew James had the real gift for spotting the exact stone for the right spot.

James would smile at his daddy, lean back, trowel pointed down on the mortar board, "Well, he got it from one of us."

Their second son, Huey, was slight like his dad and two years behind Dewayne. If there was a keyboard to be had, Huey would sit and peck out songs by ear. He wasn't five years old by the time he could play two or three songs all the way through.

"This on' ain't gonna be a mason I don't think, Momma," James said to Claudine. They asked Ruby if she might work with him or if she might recommend someone else. By then, Ruby had both a piano and organ at home. There were also various other instruments around Ira and Ruby's house for any interested. Their girls never seemed too interested, but the first time Huey got on the organ bench with his Aunt Ruby, he grinned from ear to ear as she pulled different stops as he played. After his sixth birthday they started twice-weekly lessons. Huey would come over every afternoon after school for thirty minutes to practice. A year later, Ruby was adding in a third lesson a week just on music theory. He couldn't yet reach the pedals but he had no problem navigating the two bottom manuals on the organ. On his eighth birthday, Ruby organized the first recital for Huey. Vivian and Joab's invitation got lost between the kitchen table and the mailbox, but everyone else was there, and Huey had on a nice suit and bow tie. He introduced each piece and would go back and forth between the piano and organ.

In introducing the last piece he went back to the organ and announced, "Now everyone stand and sing along as I play this final piece." He spun around on the organ bench and played the introduction to *It Is Well with My Soul*.

The house was filled with music of such joy, no heavenly choir had anything on the Jemisons that afternoon, but it didn't stop Momma Daisy saying, "Huey-boy, we'd all better do that one more time and this time like we mean it."

Trailing Huey by three years was the baby of the family, Martha Marie. She was a scrappy-thing, and the only one of the children interested in sports at school. To her it didn't matter the sport. She liked soccer, tennis and basketball. In high school, she even tried to get a girls wrestling team started; but the administration claimed, for liability reasons, they couldn't allow it.

Claudine was athletic herself so she was glad to see her daughter had similar interests. Claudine's read of the "liability concern" was the principal not wanting to hear from parents nagging him about girls not knowing their place—no doubt an opinion he shared but wouldn't come right out and say. This was the general consensus of the Jemisons as well. Tyler joked that they could call Vivian's girls and start their own squad. That this was a bad idea was the general consensus of the Jemisons as well, and so Martha Marie stuck to her three main sports. It's hard to say which she excelled at most. If there was team, it didn't take long for her to be made captain. She loved to play for the sake of the game and was less concerned about competition. She had a basketball coach who arrived her junior year when Martha Marie had been selected captain the year before as a sophomore—which was unprecedented —and he was immediately inclined to replace her with a senior.

He also took the approach of shaming them into fighting for a win every time they went on the court—hollering as much as possible in the process. Momma Daisy's straight-forward approach wasn't lost on Martha Marie. One day at practice as she was dribbling down the court, the coach started hollering wildly at one of the girls who missed a block as Martha Marie drove to the net. Instead of making the basket as she surely would have, she instead stopped in her tracks, walked over to the coach, handed him the ball and without saying a word, walked into the locker room.

The new coach screamed at her as she went, "DON'T YOU WALK AWAY FROM ME!"

She kept right on as slowly, one by one, so did the rest of the team. He was left on the empty court holding the ball with no one to shame into fighting for victory. The principal heard about it soon enough and called the coach into his office—the same principal concerned about girl wrestling liability which he had nixed the year before. He knew the Jemison force the new coach had run up against.

"Sit down, coach." As the coach sat, the principal rose and paced back and forth slowly behind him. "Ms. Jemison is a born leader and there is no better athlete in this school—boy or girl. As the story has come to me from several of her teammates—she has not been to see me—she proved to you who is captain of that team. And you have, by all accounts, proved yourself to be an ass. I suggest you find another way or another job. Which of those you choose at this point remains up to you. Choose to ignore either of these and you'll be out at the end of the school year without a recommendation from this principal. That will be all."

With that he opened the door waiting for the coach to get up and leave. It was clear he didn't want to hear any excuses or even an apology. It was up to the coach to clean up his own mess with the team.

The assistant principal was a friend of Claudine's. When she recounted all that had happened, Claudine said Martha Marie had never even mentioned what she'd done walking off the court and hadn't said much about the coach one way or the other up to that point. The account humored Claudine greatly. The assistant principal wondered what Claudine was going to say to her daughter.

"That's easy. 'You go girl!'"

The Episcopal church in Macon where the family attended had a fine pipe organ. By the time Huey was sixteen, he played something most Sundays and quickly worked up to where he could do the entire service from prelude to postlude. His early playing by ear also gave him a natural gift of improvisation. He would love to launch into a short but rafter-raising interlude as the congregation went into the last verse of the opening and closing hymns. Ruby got busy for his eighteenth birthday to arrange a Sunday afternoon recital at the Cathedral in Atlanta. There was an excellent turnout. All the Jemisons were there, of course. The invitation to Vivian and Joab was lost between the kitchen table and the mailbox. As he had done at his first recital, he introduced each piece. By now, not only could he reach the peddles and all four manuals, his fingers and feet would fly as there seemed to be no piece he could not master.

When it was time for the final piece he stood and said, "Now this last piece is a hymn which is not in the Episcopal hymnal for reasons not known. You will find the words on the back of your program, and because my grandmother is here we will be singing through this twice, the second time like we mean it. I will play an interlude between the two."

Telling Episcopalians to stand for a hymn is not needed. All stood, and with that he spun around on the organ bench and started playing—*It Is Well with My Soul*.

There was no question that Dewayne and Martha Marie would each have a good church wedding with Huey at the organ—that is, if they wanted to stay in the family will. Both happened to marry Catholics which prompted Momma Daisy to suggest, "We might be gettin'a bit *too* ecumenical in this family." Both families stayed in the Episcopal church and as Momma Daisy felt her own church movin' away from her, she used Huey's playing as a convenient justification for visiting the Episcopalians with greater frequency.

Dewayne and Marsha had two boys, and Martha Marie and John had two girls. Huey went off to get his degree in music and quite literally travels all over the world giving organ concerts and playing with renowned symphonies. Still, as often as possible, he is at the church in Macon, "Shakin' the rafters and any Episcopalians that get in his way," as his daddy liked to say.

Tragically, James died at age 53. He was running to the masonry supply store to get some more mortar when a cement truck ran a stop sign—hitting him broadside. To Tyler and no doubt to others of the family, the Jemisons seem to have had more than their share of grief and troubles. It just seems to pile up on some families.

One thing was for sure; they weren't going to go off blindly to war. It's hard to say Momma Daisy, Pappy and the rest had all become pacifists. To Tyler, that didn't seem the right term. But there was a decided firmness against war. And he did know they all lived by Momma's directive, "There ain't no boy or girl in this family gonna go off and die for some president and the rich men that pull his strings. If somebody come marchin' into Georgia, we'll decide then what to do."

Chapter Fourteen

Uncle James' untimely death caught all the family off guard. Momma Daisy and Pappy had buried the dog tag of one son, and now were about to bury their second. This would be their first funeral in an Episcopal church where baptism and confirmation were prerequisites to membership.

One thing Momma Daisy and Pappy agreed upon as pertained to the Church of God was the practice of not having church membership. "If we're the family of God, you don't need no letter saying so." While the church did do immersion baptism, it was a kind of testimony or profession and had nothing to do with making one a member. If someone happened to be sprinkled in some other church, the Church of God didn't look on that like it mattered. They considered you baptized. Momma Daisy and Pappy also liked that the church had a long history of black churches and white churches and some in between. They had, from the start, allowed women a voice in the church ordaining them, though not as common as men, of course. The Macon church hadn't yet had a woman minister, but it had plenty of women head of various committees as well as leading the singing and so forth. Momma Daisy had been called on numerous times to lead the main prayer of the service.

Every year the Church of God held an annual camp meeting in Anderson, Indiana, when people from all over the world would come for a week of singing, preaching and taking care of the business of the church. Whoever happened to be the minister in Macon was always expected to make the trip to Anderson each June. A few others from time to time would go up as well. A couple of years after the Anderson choir had been to Macon, Momma Daisy and Pappy decided to finally make the pilgrimage to camp meeting. They told the minister of their intentions, asking him if he could suggest places to stay. He offered to reserve a room for them when he booked his own motel room. They wanted to be sure it had two beds since Tyler was going to go along with them.

They'd planned all this a year ahead to be sure they'd have a room. When the time came, the minister offered to take them along with him and the Mrs., but Pappy figured this was more out of obligation than any hope that they'd actually take him up on his offer.

Momma Daisy wasn't interested, "With the three of us trying to get in the back seat of his Chevy, poor Tyler won't have an inch of wiggle room."

Pappy added, "And we might wanna talk about some'in' other than religion for all those hours. He'll think he's gotta sound holy goin' and comin'."

Pappy did all the driving. It was twelve hours with a stop or two but Pappy wanted to make it in one day each way. Tyler liked to read so he brought a couple books to keep himself occupied. Momma Daisy also used those books to her pleasure as she asked Tyler to read aloud to them. He read beyond his grade and was good at reading aloud. Pappy didn't like driving with the radio on so they had conversations going up about what each expected the days in Anderson would be like, how pretty the drive was in different spots and Tyler's reading. The ride home would be what they thought of Anderson and camp meeting, how pretty the drive was in different spots and Tyler's reading. Particular sights out the car preempted all else when one or the other saw something they thought needed calling out. Mamma Daisy loved the long distance views that some of the mountain drive afforded. She surmised how beautiful that drive would be with some fall color. Pappy loved seeing fields with the winding rows that followed the sculpted hills and the bright green flat bottom-lands. He particularly liked the tobacco fields they saw going through Kentucky. Tyler could spot little streams and waterfalls and hawks and even spotted a pheasant in Indiana.

Momma said, "Tyler-boy, for spottin' things an eagle ain't got nottin' on you."

When they got to the motel on the south edge of Anderson, Momma Daisy took one look at the two double beds and said, "Pappy, I think you bes' sleep with Tyler unless you want me rollin' you off on the floor in the night. They didn't get carried away with these beds."

With one look at the bathroom Pappy warned, "They didn't get carried away in here either." That little donut-hole seat looked mighty cramped there between the vanity and tub. He hoped she could manage it. She could—just barely.

When they got to the campus where camp meeting is held, all three thought it was as pretty a campus as any they'd ever seen. The big church at the end of the street, Park Place, with its steeple lined up perfect as you went down the hill, really caught their eye. They stopped to see if the church was unlocked. It was. They stared at the tall windows and white shutters and admired the large stained glass window up over the baptismal pool. Pappy went up for a closer look with Tyler following right behind. The pool was empty and the two went around to the side and came back out where the big organ console sat. Opposite the organ was a big Baldwin concert grand piano. There was a huge pulpit rising up over the pews. Tyler stepped into it, and you could just see the top of his head.

Momma Daisy said to the boy, "You'll have to do some more growin' up before you can preach from that mighty pulpit."

They were at every service over at the Warner Auditorium throughout the days with the thousands of other Church of God brothers and sisters. There was singing at each service, but by far the favorite service of all three of the Jemisons was the hymn sing.

We're a happy pilgrim band, Dwelling in the holy land...

This is my song, O God of all the nations, A song of peace for lands afar and mine...

Let us sing the name of Jesus, oh, that name we love so dear! Sweetest anthem earth or heaven ever breathed on mortal ear...

I will sing, hallelujah, for there's joy in the Lord, And He fills my heart with rapture as I rest on His Word...

What a mighty God we serve! What a mighty God we serve! Reigning now above, on His throne of love, What a mighty God we serve!

O Church of God, the day of jubilee has dawned so bright and glorious for thee...

Toward the end they started some of the softer hymns.

Dear Lord and Father of mankind, Forgive our foolish ways; Reclothe us in our rightful mind, In purer lives Thy service find, In deeper rev'rence, praise...

More love to Thee, O Christ. More love to Thee...

Abide with me; fast falls the eventide; The darkness deepens; Lord, with me abide...

Momma Daisy thought these were a good benediction to the day. On the drive back to the motel, she sang in her deep contralto voice that last verse again.

I fear no foe, with Thee at hand to bless: Ills have no weight, and tears no bitterness: Where is death's sting? where, grave, thy victory? I triumph still, if Thou abide with me.

Having sung it once by herself she instructed Tyler and Pappy saying, "I'll sing that verse one more time and I expect to hear two Jemison men join in."

Tyler took note that this was the first time she'd ventured into lumping him in the category of men. Just a couple days ago he was Tyler-boy. He felt all grown up all of a sudden even if he was nigh unto ten years old. The men did join as prayerfully as she had sung it the first time through. During the last few minutes of their short drive, all three sat in perfect silence—the peace of the night resting quietly in each heart.

The next day there were still some activities going on, but the highlight for the Jemisons had passed. On the drive back to Macon they were talking about how much they enjoyed some of the preaching and all of the singing. Tyler imagined that he might one day go to Anderson to college and sing in the choir at that big Park Place church. However, Pappy and Momma Daisy also had some troubling moments while they were there. They knew of plenty of churches in Macon where people tried to make things political. Neither thought this belonged in God's church no matter the

95

denomination. To that point they'd never seen the Church of God as one of those churches. Some of the decisions made that year troubled them—especially Momma Daisy.

"The Church of God had sense enough from its start not to say who could or couldn't be a member," she started out. "And now they're passin' resolutions sayin' certain ones can't have any leadership role in the church. They're worried about what some of 'em might be doing in their bedrooms. It's the Baptists that worry about such things. We ain't got no business tellin' who is in and who is out."

Tyler had some idea of the ones the leadership was worried about but didn't fully know. He just listened to Momma and Pappy, filing it all away as was his nature, for when he would call upon the memories again to help him ponder through a present situation.

Pappy didn't disagree with her. When it came to sortin' out religion, they were nearly always of one mind. Tyler sometimes thought Momma's mind, but Pappy did his own thinking, and Tyler figured he pulled Momma along as much as she pulled him along. Neither one was for standin' still.

Pappy expressed his thoughts on it, "They'd do well to reflect on that hymn we sung. *Dear Lord and Father of mankind, Forgive our foolish ways; Reclothe us in our rightful mind, In purer lives Thy service find.* They got young men and women that wanta serve and are being told, 'We don't want you.' Maybe I'm missin' the problem, but that don't seem right."

"They'll still take their money anytime the offering plate is passed," Momma Daisy figured.

Pappy speculated, "Not only take their money, but they'll hope them in their choirs don't leave. As long as they know their place ain't in the pulpit or on the payroll they'll look the other way. We know well enough what it's like for others to think we oughta know our place and keep it."

They both had about all of that they wanted to think about at the moment. Momma Daisy capped it off with this, "It's a sad day when the Church of God start dividin' us up. It's a sad day."

That made something pop into Tyler's mind in response, "We got glad days because we got each other. We don't need them makin' sad days for us."

"Young man, where did you get so wise?" Pappy asked. "Must be from your pappy, don't you reckon?"

"Momma done some of the work too," Tyler replied, and all three had a good laugh just as they went by a Kentucky tobacco field.

"Oh, that's pretty," Pappy said. And all went quiet for a long time. Tyler recalled his pappy's words again. It was the second time he'd been called a man.

Huey played the lead role in planning his father James's service. He talked to his mother, Claudine, and Momma Daisy about scriptures and hymns. A lot of Momma Daisy's favorite hymns weren't in the Episcopal hymnal, but she attended enough services that she had learned several of their favorite hymns. Several she liked. And she was often surprised that some of the hymns she did know from the Church of God had more verses in the Episcopal hymnal and that Episcopalians sing every verse, which she approved of with one caveat.

She'd say, "Huey, good thing you got that organ stirrin' things up for all those verses or that crowd would fall asleep on their feet. Our Church of God could sure teach them folk some proper singin'."

It was true. For all the love of music in the Episcopal church, James and his family could never quite understand how so many could stand like pillars during those hymns. The Jemison pew could be heard around the sanctuary and they always had a handful of others trying to join them.

Momma Daisy was sure when the church was full of everyone who knew James, that Episcopal church would be filled with voices like never before.

Claudine deferred to Huey for hymn suggestions and to Momma Daisy for scriptures. Claudine said that since many attending wouldn't be Episcopalian, she thought it best if they didn't have communion since most wouldn't come forward even if invited. They looked at the scripture selections noted in the Book of

Common Prayer. Momma Daisy reviewed the list and wanted to include one of her favorite passages not on the list, Luke 6:27-38. This, she said, represented the way Christians ought to be living adding, "If we can skip over the creed I wouldn't mind. It ain't that I don't believe it. I just think we need to profess our love instead of a list of propositions that ain't changin' hearts."

Huey would take the results of their planning to the priest to see if she would agree. What they decided was a hymn in place of the Old Testament reading, Psalm 23, I Corinthians 13, the passage from Luke, no creed. The hymns were to be, *All Creatures of our God and King*, which was Claudine's favorite, *Lift High the Cross*, *Come Thou Fount of Every Blessing* and *Abide with Me*. Those were all in the hymnal. *It Is Well with My Soul* was not. *Lift High the Cross* is one Momma Daisy learned from the Episcopalians and she deemed it one of the finest hymns she'd ever heard.

She said to Huey and Claudine, "If I had a favorite from that hymnal of yours, of the ones I've learned so far, that would be it."

Huey took the plan to the priest. He also told her that he was going to try to get a small group of men to sing an arrangement he'd done of *It Is Well with My Soul*, that they would sing a cappella at the graveside if that would be okay. If he couldn't get a group together, he would sing it as a solo, inviting any who wanted to join in. Huey was eager to try out the three-part men's arrangement of the song he'd completed just a few weeks earlier.

The priest was fine with the plans for the graveside. She was a bit concerned about skipping the creed and communion. As Huey and Claudine both knew, if she was leading the service, communion was sure to follow. She was not like some Episcopal clergy who would go back and forth between morning prayer and the eucharist.

Huey's approach to resolution was to lay out what Claudine and Momma Daisy had said about both adding, "You've met my grandmother. Would you like to challenge her on why they must be included in the service?"

The priest conceded, "No creed, no communion. Huey, it will be a beautiful service. Thank you for coordinating things with your family."

This was Momma Daisy and Pappy's first Episcopal funeral. The casket was under a pall in the front of the church. No last minute viewing. The family would normally wait to be seated and come in all together as at most churches. However, Claudine, Momma Daisy and Pappy all wanted to be in the church for Huey's prelude. So, before most arrived, all the family was already seated in the front pews. Huey played a couple short pieces for them that was not part of his prelude. When the first persons were seated, he started in with an improvisation of hymns in the Church of God hymnal that were not in the Episcopal hymnal. He was sure to include any that he knew to be a favorite of anyone in the family. He finished with *It Is Well with My Soul*. As he could do with no seeming effort, he could extend as long as needed or cut off as needed. Anyone listening would guess he had it all perfectly timed.

He stopped playing. The bell was rung a number of times. The crucifer started slowly down the aisle with the priest following as all turned to face the aisle. The priest started the liturgy.

I am the resurrection and the life, saith the Lord;
he that believeth in me, though he were dead, yet shall he live;
and whosoever liveth and believeth in me shall never die.

I know that my Redeemer liveth,
and that he shall stand at the latter day upon the earth;
and though this body be destroyed, yet shall I see God;
whom I shall see for myself and mine eyes shall behold,
and not as a stranger.

For none of us liveth to himself,
and no man dieth to himself.
For if we live, we live unto the Lord.
and if we die, we die unto the Lord.
Whether we live, therefore, or die, we are the Lord's.

Blessed are the dead who die in the Lord;
even so saith the Spirit, for they rest from their labors.

The service over, the burial done, the fellowship meal complete, the Jemisons met back at Momma Daisy and Pappy's. Even Vivian came with Billy, the youngest, in tow. They were the only Washingtons to bother coming to the service. The whole tribe had made an obligatory passing through the funeral home visitation, but couldn't be bothered further. Billy seemed behaved at the funeral home, the church and now at Momma and Pappy's. Might this one be redeemable? It was the first encouraging sign any had ever seen from the Washington mess. They would have to come up with a plan to save the child from an otherwise cloudy future.

Momma Daisy called Ira, Tyler and Pappy to come into the kitchen. She had something to say. Just as she got to the door she turned to say, "Huey, you come too, boy."

When all were assembled, Pappy asked, "What is it, Mother?"

Tyler, and no doubt Ira or Huey, had never heard him call her "Mother" before. He just always called her Daisy or even Momma like the rest of the bunch.

She started in, "Unless my husband of these many years stipulates otherwise, which he can do right now or later as he sees fit, that is the service I would like for him and for me. Hopefully, those Episcopalians will see us out even if we aren't members. You know we don't believe in membership of churches, but that was the most beautiful funeral I've ever been to. Huey, you did a lot to make your daddy's funeral special, especially them men you sang with at the grave. That was beautiful. I hope you will set it all up the same for me and for Pappy."

Huey couldn't have answered if he wanted to. For the first time since James had died he broke into tears. Momma Daisy went to the boy and held him tight and Pappy hugged the two of them. Ira put his arm around Tyler and they wept for James, for themselves, and for the love that held them all together.

As Tyler would account after both had passed, the Episcopalians did see them out, and it was no small shock from the Church of God minister and others in the church that they didn't have their funeral "in their own church." Pappy never suggested a single change to the service, and Huey saw to it they each got the send-off Momma Daisy wanted.

There was one difference for both from Uncle James' funeral. Dewayne organized a big shrimp and crab boil for both Pappy and Momma Daisy's funerals. The sun shone bright on both days, and they moved the tables and chairs out onto the lawn of the church. The men left their coats and ties in the parish hall and rolled up their sleeves. Dewayne had plastic seafood bibs for everyone. Dewayne was the master of the grill and boiling pot for the Jemisons. He could manage any size crowd. He went from table to table checking on everyone. If he saw anyone cuttin' corners he'd say in his big bass voice, "That ain't no way to eat crab. Some Cajun gonna come along and snatch up what you're throwing out and show you how it's done."

Chapter Fifteen

Tyler heard enough radio and television to know that the way the Jemison family communicated wasn't exactly the same English. Once Tyler started school, he found out real quick that the way he talked was not allowed in class. Tyler was always a book lover, and in the books he read there were many who wrote like the Jemisons talked. He heard the same kind of language in some of the movies he'd seen in the theatre. When others were still learning to read, he'd already read about Huck Finn and his friend Jim. He was a little surprised by the fact that the teacher was so determined they stick to TV and Radio English.

Having thorough instructions from Momma Daisy and Pappy to always be respectful and to do as the teacher asked, he took his curiosity about this back to them. Before going to them, he first thought it over in his own mind for a few weeks. Then one night at supper, Pappy's prayer prompted the boy to bring it up.

Pappy didn't like memorized prayers and changed them up some to fit what was on his mind. That evening it was, "Lord, we give you powerful thanks for the feast Momma and you done set here for the boy and me. We need it to give us the strength to git past them that don't know the love you wanna pour down on 'em, causin' 'em to live in hate from one day to the next. They need the food that's made in love and the love that is the food to git us all by. Help us give 'em that love—wantin' it or not. In Jesus name. Ay-men."

Momma would always add her own, "Ay-men!"

When the prayer went along this line of thought, Tyler figured Pappy had had a hard day at work or run into somebody particularly unpleasant—maybe Joab. Before Pappy and Uncle James had struck out on their own, there was one man on the mason crew who stirred such prayers in Pappy. He had a foul mouth and foul temper and as Pappy had said a time or two, "He thinks it's a gift to share with the rest of us." When trying to explain the man to Tyler he once said, "He's a man who lives only by pride and since he's got nothin' to be properly proud of, it makes for an angry, hateful man." Tyler learned from his Uncle James years later that the man was white and had tended mason for

Pappy. This to Uncle James' mind would make it all clear to Tyler why the man carried such hate. Tyler wondered why the man didn't get fired.

James replied, "Because his daddy owned the company and he ain't never gonna be a mason because he ain't got the patience or the brains to learn to butter up a brick and his daddy knows it."

Tyler started in. "Pappy, that was a real nice prayer. My teacher is on me and the kids in the class to talk like they do on TV, proper English as she calls it. She'd be correctin' that prayer a yours. You graduated high school. Was things different back then?"

Momma and Pappy saw the boy had been givin' this some consideration.

"It was the same way back in the dark ages, boy," Pappy said. "The way my daddy explained it to me was the teacher needed to find common ground for the children—thems born there and thems moved in from other places. He said people comin' from different places bring with 'em their own dialect. That's a word that just means people adapted words to suit amongst themselves. There ain't nothin' wrong with using proper English and there ain't nothin' wrong using the dialect."

This was a start but led Tyler to the first problem with it. "But everyone in the class is from Macon and all talk like we do here at home. You know, for a fact, so is the teacher. She grew up in our church."

Momma made a run at it this time, "But she still gotta teach like the other Georgia teachers if she wanna keep her job. You don't want her losin' her job over not making you boys and girls use proper English, do you?"

Tyler, never one to lie responded, "Some days it seems like a good idea."

And as they were moved to do on so many occasions before, both laughed at the boy's honest and natural gift for humorin' 'em.

Pappy said, "Your momma should have kept those essays she wrote in high school. You'd see she had mastered proper English as good as any college professor. I never did near as well as her, but always did enough to pass. You gotta remember too, neither one of us know that many people who did graduate or ever did very good in school. It ain't ours to lord over them our education. You just remember, do like your teacher wants in school. You might need a job where the only way to get it is to know proper English. In the end you will know two languages. One that requires everything just so, and one that don't. What do you make of that, Tyler-boy?"

Tyler thought he had the perfect response, "Ain't ain't a word 'cause the teacher said it ain't, but the teacher ain't always right."

Momma chuckled and said, "Close enough, Tyler-boy."

Pappy added his frequent observation to something Tyler said or observed, "You're smarter than the average bear."

It all made sense to Tyler now, and his years in school would favor Momma's skill for speaking and writing proper English when such was called for, and not lording his education over others. He genuinely loved the mastery of English poetry at its highest art. And he equally loved fittin' with the freer tongue of his upbringing. He was intent on making sure his boys appreciated that there was one that requires everything just so, and one that don't.

I understood all this as well. My own upbringing was a mix of Swiss dialect phrases that my grandmother used with great frequency, and my mother repeated them even though, often as not, she couldn't translate them. She just knew them as expressions that seemed to fit particular situations. For sure they were pure dialect and not high German. I tried to find translations myself for those phrases I remembered and could only find them to some near approximation. And on the farm we had no problem with words like "ain't." My Mennonite father even liked the word "shit" pretty well. There were few contexts other than Sunday morning church where it seemed out of place to work in. He did know where to draw the line. I knew boys in school who said their dads said they had shit for brains. That was not something a good Mennonite or any good dad would ever say to his children. Dad knew shit belonged for spreadin' but not on your kids.

When I left Indiana after graduating college, I found myself in the South where dialects I'd only heard in movies were prevalent. My ear goes naturally to the voices around it. It didn't take any time before y'all and fixin' were as natural to me as any boy who grew up in the South. Before working for the university, I also worked in construction while getting my bachelor's and master's, thanks to the useful skills of my Mennonite roots. The crew in Baton Rouge had a number of black men who I respected as much as anyone in the world. For whatever reason, they talked in my presence as though I'd spent my whole life with them. I loved the freedom of their own dialect and their free tongue about their encounters with—what would have to be described as anything but charitable—white Christians. Soon enough, I found myself totally bilingual between, as Tyler's pappy had put it, "one that requires everything just so and one that don't."

Part IV

Chapter Sixteen

Tyler and the boys had already checked out of the hotel. When they left the Daisy Cafe, they were ready for the six-plus-hour trip back to Macon. How long would depend on the number of stops along the way. How many stops would depend on the boys. Tyler was still working out the extraordinary days in Boone and could have easily just driven in complete silence, stopping only long enough to fill-up the one time required. The boys had been on their best behavior and a silent drive was the furthest thing from their mind. They were wound up and with good reason. They were ready to imagine their life in Boone, and wanted their daddy to lay out what happens between gettin' back to Macon and drivin' to their new home in Boone and how they get in their new school and where would they go to church and...and...and. Tyler could see this was going to be 325 miles of Q&A. With questions coming at him as fast as the stripes on the highway, Tyler decided to take a sequential and as detailed an approach as possible to answer the boys' questions.

Tyler liked to work in quotes from literature whenever he could that he knew the boys had heard. "Listen my children and you shall hear of the midnight drive of Tyler Revere."

The two boys responded in unison, "On the eighteenth of April in seventy-five. Hardly a man is now alive."

They half expected their daddy to continue with the next line but instead he said, "We can't quite align the dates, but we will remember this famous date and year, when two boys with their daddy felt Momma Daisy's hand working some amazing wonders for her boys."

Tyler said, "On the ride home, I want you each to make a list of the things you think you want to take along with us to Boone. I think we will follow Mr. August's suggestion and not worry about bringing anything big. We clearly don't need it there, and if we get around to buying a house at some point we'd probably mostly want to start over anyway. The city offered some moving expense money, but nothing we have would add up to using that money and storing what we have to make it worth the expense. My first act as city manager, even before I start the job, will be to spare them my moving expenses. When you each get your list worked out, I want you to give it to your brother and see if he agrees. When you got it all worked out, then you can read out your list to me.

"But before you start that, let's cover some of your questions. I'm sure there is information online about getting registered for school. I'll look at that first thing when we get home. The family has given us time since Momma Daisy died for us to work out where we were going to live so we can get the old house on the market. I'll see if they want us to sell the furniture or try to sell the house with it furnished. All that furniture isn't really mine to move anyway, though they always assumed I would end up with it. Except for Momma's rocker. That, for sure, needs to go back to Uncle Ira, and who he chooses to pass it on to is up to him since he made it."

"All three of us could sit in it," Johnny said, pleased with having thought of it.

Tyler went on with his thoughts, "It really helps having a place to live all lined up already. I can get all the forms filled out that I need to for car insurance and to get my North Carolina driver's license as soon as we get there. I want to get that taken care of before I start work, if possible, as I'm sure I'll need it for any city-owned vehicles I might need to drive. It looks like we should be able to get there a week to ten days before I start work, so that is going to make it a lot easier to ease into things.

"Now as for church, I don't have any idea. Congregations are funny things. Just because the sign out front says 'welcome' doesn't necessarily mean it's so. And just because it says Church of God out front doesn't mean it's gonna feel like Momma and Pappy's church. In fact, I know you heard Momma Daisy say she felt more and more like the church, to use her words, 'was walkin' away from her—judgin' where they ought not be judgin' and more worried about the carpet than the poor.'"

Johnny piped in, "And she sure didn't like it that they stopped singing the old hymns."

Tyler agreed, "You're right! She said the only time she heard her favorite hymns anymore was when somebody old died and they'd left, as she put it, 'proper instructions.' She thought that ought to tell the minister that they weren't doing right by their elders. She said he was more worried about what robe made him look pretty."

"She said he liked to play dress-up when he was called to dress-down," Jimmy added.

Tyler was always amazed at how much those boys picked up and remembered. He thought most such things passed over young boys like so much hot air, but if it was something Momma or Pappy said, they were always listening and filing it away. Tyler was relieved Momma wasn't a gossip. No telling what news around town they might have recalled if such was the case. As it was, her most critical viewpoints were reserved for clergy and politicians and for the same reasons. "They's to be servants, not masters."

Johnny recalled that Pappy would add, "And a lot of people with master's degrees think it makes them one."

Tyler clarified the record a bit. "Pappy was all for education. He just thought somewhere along the line they forgot all about humility. When I started work on my master's he told me, 'I'm glad to see you continue your learning, but if you get a master's and then a doctorate and think that makes you high and mighty, then I'll know somewhere along the line Momma and I failed you.' I told Pappy, if I ever commit that sin it won't be yours or Momma's failing. That one would be squarely on me. He said back to me, 'Well, the fact you know it would be a sin tells me I probably don't need to fret about you.' Remember that, boys."

Johnny was at the age he liked to work in expressions he'd heard. He thought he had a workable solution to offer on the church situation. "I think when we get to Boone we might try the bedside Baptists."

"You have a natural gift for sleeping in, I'll grant that. It wouldn't take any effort from you. I'd be more inclined to being a backyard-barbecue Baptist myself. How about you, Jimmy?"

"That sounds a lot better than sleepin' all day."

Johnny said, "I can stand in the backyard and sing, *All Things Bright and Beautiful*. Momma and Pappy would like that."

"Yes they would. They both said you sing like an angel."

"That's cause I am an angel."

Tyler caught that one, "Johnny, what did we just say about losing humility? As for your angelic status, you know how to be one when you wanna be. You just don't always wanna be."

Clearly he was in an angelic mood at the moment. He didn't respond. He just sat back in the seat, stared out the window and sang—*All things bright and beautiful, all creatures great and small, all things wise and wonderful, the lord God made them all...* Jimmy joined in on the parts he knew. Tyler just listened as he always did when the boys sang. For whatever unknown synapse caused this, Tyler was waiting to see if this song led to one Johnny often followed up with, which to Tyler's mind had no viable connection to whatever had come before. He did. There was only the briefest pause when he launched into a rousing—*Kids under construction maybe the paint is still wet. Kids under construction the Lord might not be finished yet...* Jimmy quickly joining in. As they got into it, Tyler softly said to himself in an almost sudden ping of melancholy, "Kids, and all the rest of us."

Jimmy had his own finale to kick off when they had exhausted the "kids" song. He started in—*It is the song that never ends, and it goes on and on my friends, someone—started singing it not knowing what it was and they'll continue singing it forever just because...* Johnny and Tyler joined in for the repeat, and the repeat after that, and thank goodness found an end after all when it was time for a fill-up and pit-stop.

With the tank topped up and all three with a fountain drink, a bag of cashews and some local-homemade venison jerky that the station had, the Jemison boys were back on the road. Tyler suggested it was time to work on their lists. He wanted some relative quiet, especially since that melancholy was back as his thoughts were taken to what brought them to a father raising two boys on his own, and what that meant for him, and what it must mean for those two in the back seat. To this point the boys knew virtually nothing about why things were the way they were, though he knew the time was coming close to when they would have to talk about it. He didn't see any way of easing into it with Johnny only to wait three more years to tell the same to Jimmy—thus it was just easier to try to wait until Tyler thought both boys could begin to comprehend. That was the best hope he had—trying to feed them bits and pieces of all that needed to be given them.

He also knew he would need three versions of the story. The first gradual story would be for the boys. A second telling was what he would want to tell me at some point, and anyone with whom he would be close to—including a possible spouse. The third version more general in nature. How to explain his situation to co-workers and the curious who ask about his personal life. He'd already dealt with this a bit, but moving to a new place where no one knew him or his family history would ratchet up the frequency and depth of the conversation beyond a level he wasn't used to having to deal with. This was the one dread he had about leaving the known world of his life in Macon.

The boys already knew that their mother, Mariah Winters— she kept her maiden name—lives in Boquete, Panama. That she left when Jimmy was just two years old makes him rather oblivious to life without her. Johnny, of course, remembers her, but Tyler has done everything possible to never talk as though she is to blame, is a bad person, or that the boys in any way are the reason she is gone. They get a birthday card and Christmas card from her and nothing more. She has never called and claims not to have a phone. This may be true. Tyler didn't know any different. She has never asked for a divorce and Tyler hasn't forced one—easy enough for him given her residence in a foreign country. She was a Macon native, but Tyler knows that she has a permanent residency visa in Panama. Whatever she does for income is unknown to Tyler. She has never asked for any kind of support. He speculates that she co-inhabits with someone but that is mere speculation. He does know that she has even less contact with her family than she does with the two boys. Her father told Tyler they've never heard from her from the day she got on the plane in Atlanta. Her parents have since moved to Dallas and Tyler never hears from them either. The boys sign a mother's day card that Tyler suggests is a kind thing to do, and he mails it to the post office box she puts as her address on the cards she sends. It's an odd kind of silence that is cold and distant and surely must be resolved in some fashion at some point. His melancholy mood and the account that would be needed in meeting new people led him to think he ought to file for divorce, and let her live her life and the boys theirs, without any lingering custody claims. He'd long been persuaded that it seemed improbable that she would seek any custody arrangement, and if she did he would fight it. But he also wanted any divorce to give her some right to visitation if she wanted it. He didn't want his boys wondering someday, asking why he would restrict even the most basic social connection. There was nothing in her behavior that suggested to him that they needed to fear her in any way.

For someone who didn't rush into marriage, and for someone who can't imagine his own life without the boys, he also knows he should not have married when he did to whom he did. It was a relationship that was rather static, which is hardly an endorsement for lifetime vows. He's often assumed they married just because everyone kept asking when they would and both were tired of dodging the question. Momma Daisy never asked the question or drilled Tyler about it once the engagement and wedding date were announced. Tyler took this as a tacit sign that she understood better than he what the underlying flaw in their relationship was, but even someone as bold and fearless as she just didn't know how to talk about it. He figured what she couldn't talk about she prayed about, and he never doubted she prayed for Tyler and Mariah. When the boys came along she accepted them as hers, just as she had Tyler when his daddy was killed and his momma left.

Keeping the occasional eye on the boys in the back seat, he could see they had exchanged lists and some whispered comments were going back and forth. They could tell their daddy was staring down the road, his mind on his list, they assumed.

Tyler asked, "How are you coming with those lists?"

"Pretty good, I think," Johnny said.

"Jimmy, let me hear what you've come up with. Are these in order of importance or just a list?"

Jimmy said, "The most important first. 1) my legos and transformers, 2) my computer, 3) my clothes, 4) all our books.

Tyler was pleased with the practicality of the list, if not its priority order, and asked Johnny for his. He always thought Johnny, like him, was a big picture kind of thinker. For his age, it often surprised him with what could only be described as delight in the young thinker.

He started in, "Jimmy said all the books so I put all the music and movies on my list, plus my computer, plus some of our games if there is room. We also made a list of things there's no point moving. We should just buy new when we get there."

Tyler knew the brevity of the lists was too frugal to be true, "Oh, really, and what do we need not bother to move that we'll want to buy new in Boone."

Johnny served as spokesman. "No point in movin' our bikes. We both are outgrowin' the ones we got anyway. No point in moving all our clothes. We're gonna need more winter stuff and less summer stuff. Might as well start fresh. There will probably be other things where new would be better, but that's all we thought of for now."

Perhaps the boys thought the bikes would be a hard sell and lightened their list to make room for the notion. Truth was, Tyler was relieved to hear they weren't attaching to a lot of things for sentimental reasons. Since they lived in the same house all their life, he was imaging much longer lists as their minds moved from room to room. Could be, they still will do that. For now, he was delighted with their work on the project, and buying the boys new bikes and clothes was as practical as it would be fun to do as they settled in.

By Sunday, Tyler emailed me saying they'd arrived home safely and had decided to follow my suggestion on moving light. Other than a few personal items they would be bringing, they were good with the apartment as is. He also detailed the trip home, with the singing and the work on the lists. They got me singing it now! *It is the song that never ends...*

Chapter Seventeen

I didn't have much to do to get ready for the boys to move in. All the utilities were good to go. It had been two years since anyone lived there, so I checked everything out to be sure things were in working order. I looked at the old TV in the living room and decided it was pretty sorry for what people are used to these days. I had that old heavy thing hauled off and a new 55" TV installed on the wall, with a new sound system and DVD player to go with it. I debated whether to get one for each of the bedrooms and decided against it. I don't like that myself and followed the rule, do unto others as you would have them do unto you. If that's something Tyler wants, then he can buy his own. Everything else seemed up to snuff. I didn't ask if anyone played the piano, and I didn't happen to notice if they paid any particular attention to it or not. For the sake of readiness I had it tuned. It's just an upright, but it's a Yamaha and in excellent condition. Maybe it will inspire one or more of them to study piano. Like most of the contents of the apartment, they are Robert's things that we kept, reupholstering as needed and adding to modestly over the years. The furniture was of such quality that everything was solid as a rock and timeless in their classic design.

I also emailed Tyler with a basic inventory of what was in the kitchen and what tools were available to him. I know he'd looked around the kitchen pretty thoroughly, but it's hard to remember after the fact what all is there. No point in them loading a lot of pots, pans, plates and such when everything is already well stocked.

Tyler was kind enough to email me every few days with updates on how things were progressing there.

He had arranged for both Ira and James' oldest boy, Dewayne —who had been executor for James' estate—to come over on Monday night of his return to talk about Momma Daisy and Pappy's house and furnishings. Tyler laid out the situation in Boone and their intent to travel light. Tyler appreciated that as he had planned to do and did, Dewayne also deferred all decisions on the house to Ira. Most of the men in the family took more after

Pappy than Momma. The one exception to this was Dewayne. He was a big boy. The first thing Ira addressed was the chair.

"Now boys, you know I made that big oak rocker there for Momma. It lasted all her years and still don't need a thing done to it. I've always kept the finish good and made sure nothing was ever working loose. You know Momma did a heap a praying for all of us sitting in that chair. Dewayne, I want you to have it."

"Uncle Ira! I don't know what to say," Dewayne exclaimed.

"If you're gonna say anything then there's only two words to say; 'Thank you.'"

"Well, I'll make it six words then. Thank you, Uncle Ira. Thank you!"

In his matter of fact way, Ira said, "There, that's done." Then he proceeded with his ideas on everything else. "We could bring in someone who handles estate sales and just have them price everything in the house, but at 70% of what they think its value really is. Then we invite all the relatives to come and bid on anything they want starting at that 70% number. I think James' kids and grandkids and mine might want this or that. Tyler, you should speak up before then if you think of things you want. Most likely, Dewayne and I would agree to gift those prior to any sale of other things. You've already assured us there won't be a moving truck backed up here in the middle of the night.

"At the end, all the proceeds will be put back into the estate until the house is sold and then divided up according to Momma and Daddy's will. If someone in the family wants the house then we'll take sealed bids from any interested, otherwise we'll list it with a realtor.

"If there are no objections, the invitations to Vivian and Joab might get lost between the kitchen table and the mailbox." There were no objections.

For some time, Tyler had kept a set of divorce papers on hand that a lawyer from the church had drawn up. He also had a letter ready to accompany the document when he felt the time had come to proceed with trying to get Mariah to bring closure to their situation. He would update the letter to reflect their upcoming change of address.

Tyler had always blamed himself more than her for their separation. Familiarity did not translate well into intimacy, and the fact that they had two children in their short time together wasn't remarkable, but neither was it a fitting characterization of their relationship. Growing up in the church when he did was not a time of freedom, to his mind, to explore one's sexuality. Things were one way and only one way and that was that. He found it rather astounding that the two boys who came out of the marriage would be such an absolute blessing to him while their mother could coldly walk away. He had long considered himself the cold one in the relationship, and she as the one wanting and deserving an affection he just seemed incapable of offering in any authentic sense. His affections were duty and her needs real. Yet here they were—him with the boys in the same wonderful loving home that had reared him, and their mother gone to Panama with, it seemed, no love lost on Tyler, certainly, but also no love lost for the boys. This he could not comprehend and neither could Momma Daisy and Pappy.

It was such a great blessing to Tyler that they had never moved out of the home place even after they married, but maybe Mariah was partly escaping the strength of the great Jemison matriarch. If so, she never said. She seemed fine in their situation and lived under the assumption that when the two elders were gone, the house would be Tyler's. In this regard, Mariah thought of it already as their place and Momma and Pappy as the guests. With her gone, Tyler was comforted by the love the boys had for Momma and Pappy, and how easily both made it for the three of them in Mariah's absence.

It was time to get on with it. Tyler had his part of the papers notarized, and put them with his letter to Mariah regarding what he hoped would be an amicable way forward for them both. He was eager to get it sent off, as mail to Boquete wasn't necessarily an overnight process regardless of the postage paid. By the Tuesday they were back in Macon, the documents were in the mail. Now all he could do was wait. He wondered if she would call. He wondered if she would get them and just ignore them. He wondered about her just showing back up in Macon with a lawyer of her own. He waited. A few days before they were to leave for Boone, there was a large envelope with no name on the return address—just the PO box in Boquete. He carried it into the house and sat down in the living room. The boys were in the backyard. He opened it.

"Thank the lord," he whispered. She had signed it. No letter. Just the document signed and notarized. Tyler took it to his attorney who took care of what was needed to finalize everything with the court.

He was now the first divorced descendent of Ira James and Margarette Marie (Moffit) Jemison. When that thought hit him, he said out loud to himself—"Not the legacy I was hoping to pass on to my boys." The only thing left to do was figure out how to feed this latest bit to them. That, he thought, could hold until after the move.

With Dewayne as head chef, Uncle Ira organized a big-send off for Tyler, Johnny and Jimmy. They included people Tyler worked with, families of the children Johnny and Jimmy were friends with at school, people from the Church of God, Episcopal and Methodist churches who knew them in some form or fashion and every Jemison and Moffit imaginable. The invitation to Vivian and Joab even found its way to the mailbox for the first time in some time. Dewayne asked his uncle if he was sure about them getting that invitation.

Uncle Ira said, "If they come, which is a pretty big if, it gives a second chance to see if there is still some hope for that little boy, Billy. We owe it to him if not his folks."

"Fair enough," Dewayne conceded.

They arranged to hold the farewell barbecue at Central City Park. With the help of others from the family and a couple of his fellow masons, Dewayne cooked up a feast of brisket, ribs, chicken and stuffed pork loins. Uncle Ira, Aunt Ruby and Aunt Claudine purchased all the meat and everything Dewayne needed to get it cooked. Everything else was potluck.

Uncle Ira went up to Tyler and the boys. He put each arm around a boy and said, "Your Momma Daisy would be sayin' right now, 'Look at this sight, boys. These people are pouring down their love for you. I hope you can see how much love there is in the world that don't cost no money to have. It only cost bein' what the good Lord made you to be.'"

Tyler hugged his uncle with the best Momma Daisy hug his small frame could muster and said in his uncle's ear, "When I hug you, I know I'm huggin' Momma and Pappy all over again. You are the best of both of them."

Ira said, "Well I'd like to be, but I fall short plenty of times. Those is hard shoes to fill."

Tyler left it at, "Yes, they are."

The turnout was tremendous. Even the Washington mess showed up in full force. Aunt Ruby suspected of her own daughter and son-in-law that it had everything to do with all you could eat, and not anything to do with bidding Tyler and the boys a courteous farewell. This seemed only to be confirmed when Ruby asked Tyler afterwards if he'd talked to Vivian.

He said, "I saw her across the way but she never came over to speak, and I never got free enough from the crowd to make my way over to her."

Ruby thought that would be like Tyler, to put half the weight of her disrespect onto himself as not getting over to talk to her. Ruby did talk to Vivian and when she did, little Billy grabbed his grandmother, who he barely knew, and hugged both her legs. Ruby put one hand on the boy's head and said, "Vivian, if that place of yours is too crowded for number seven here, you can bring him to our house anytime. We'll be glad to take over from here."

Vivian's answer shocked her at least momentarily, "Joab would be all too glad to take you up on that. This one cries practically every time his daddy comes into the room. Joab says, 'This boy ain't no Washington! He's pure Jemison!'"

Apparently this was a bad thing. Ruby offered the only thing she could think of at the moment saying, "The offer stands. We'd go so far as adopting Billy if you and Joab were amenable to it." She was determined to rescue the boy as they all had promised to do if it was possible. A week later, Joab drove Vivian and Billy over to Ira and Ruby's, stayed in the car but honked the horn twice in quick succession, while Vivian came up the walk with a small suitcase and a small boy. She knocked on the door. Ruby opened it and looked immediately down to Billy.

Vivian proceeded, "Joab says he thinks it's best for the boy if you go ahead and adopt this one. He ain't happy at home, and when we asked him if he'd like to live with his grandma Ruby he said 'yes.' So, we've brought his clothes and hope you honor your offer to keep him."

By now, Ira was standing behind Ruby. When he heard her use the word "honor" he felt his skin crawl. He thought to himself, those two don't know the meaning of the word. Both he and Ruby at least expected Vivian to bend down to give the boy a parting kiss. As Ira moved beside Ruby in the doorway, Vivian handed him the suitcase and turned to go. Only to protect the boy did they say nothing at the time. They let her walk away from the one ray of light that had ever shown in that dark household, and they stepped aside to let that light come into their warm and loving home. Soon they completed the boy's adoption. He was to be officially, Billy Ray Jemison.

Chapter Eighteen

People had been eager to give Tyler and the boys going away gifts. The invitations to the barbecue let everyone know they were moving with minimal room for anything beyond what they already had. If any wanted to contribute to a cash gift, they were to get their donation to Uncle Ira beforehand. All were encouraged to proceed quietly so they could give the gift as a surprise. Ira, Ruby and Claudine were trusting it would be a respectable figure.

Jo Carol had been asked to give the blessing, after which she would invite her father to come forward "to say a few words."

"We gather in this park today to show our love and gratitude for your faithful servant Tyler and his boys, Johnny and Jimmy. We ask your blessing on their travels and as they make a new home in the North Carolina mountains. May all of us gathered here bear witness to the love of the faithful heritage of those who have gone before us. We especially remember Ira James, Margarette Marie, Horatio Spafford and James Martin Jemison whose lives have touched our family and our community. And bless this food that has been lovingly prepared and abundantly shared, that it may strengthen us for the trials and joys of our lives. Let us taste no bread that does not strengthen us to show thy great love and mercy. In Christ's name we pray. And all the people said,"

"Amen."

She continued, "Now before everyone runs to get in line and feast on all this delicious food, Daddy would like to say a few words."

Ira moved up a bit to stand just beside his daughter. "Tyler, Johnny, Jimmy, please come stand here by me."

They gathered themselves up and stood between Ira and Jo Carol. Ruby and Claudine stood on the opposite side of Jo Carol. Ira said, "You needn't worry about a long speech. This bunch that came here this afternoon wanted to give you a gift for your journey." He reached in his shirt pocket pulling out a check. "Here is a little traveling money." He handed Tyler a check for $3,755.

Tyler was shocked. He looked at Jimmy and Johnny and said to the crowd, "These two had suggested their old bikes stay in Georgia as they were about worn out anyway. It was their notion they get new ones when we get to North Carolina. Looks like y'all just financed two fine bikes and a heap of other things that will no doubt get us settled in. We'll sure try to honor the memory of Momma Daisy, Pappy, my daddy and Uncle James. Thank you so much. We'll never forget all you've meant to us." Laughing a bit on the verge of tears he concluded, "And I didn't think I could get all that said without breakin' down. Bless you all. Now let's see how Dewayne and his crew did on that barbecue!"

Everyone broke into applause and headed to the long table spread for all.

Tyler and the boys had loaded the U-Haul that morning. They were going to leave first thing the next morning. When they had everything loaded, they looked inside the small trailer and Tyler said, "I think maybe we packed too light. Look at all the space left over. Do you two think we need to make another round to find more to fill it up some?"

Both treated the idea as a serious notion which for Tyler wasn't really a serious question. After a minute of thinking it through Jimmy said, "Jesus told his followers not to take anything extra. I think we already got more than they ever had."

Johnny gave the order, "Pull down the door, Daddy! We're loaded and ready to go."

Tyler was glad the barbecue was an afternoon-early-evening affair. As it was, he was pretty worn out and not too eager to get up early next morning, but his two "alarm clocks" had no such problem. The boys were in rocking him back and forth saying, "Outa bed, sleepyhead. Outa bed, sleepyhead." It was clear this was going to continue until sleepyhead was up.

Tyler looked over at the clock on the dresser. 6:30. "6:30— really?"

Back came the answer to that, "Outa bed, sleepyhead."

He relented, "I'm up. I'm up."

The boys were dressed and ready to go. Tyler took a quick shower and was ready in short order. He straightened up the bathroom and whatever loose ends he saw had developed between their loading and the morning. He proposed to the boys that they'd drive a while before stopping to eat anywhere. As wound up as they were, it only made sense to head out. By 7:15 they were in the RAV4—trailer lights checked one last time—and gave a good honk as they passed the Jemison households. If any of them were up, they weren't on their porches to wave them off. He knew they would recognize his horn and was content to just keep going. It would have only been harder if they were all standing outside waiting for them to pass.

Tyler knew pulling the trailer would add at least an hour to their trip and figured closer to two. He made sure the boys had some books—including their blank sketch books, crayons and colored pencils—so they could keep themselves occupied. They wasted no time retreating into their own imaginations, each one's head moving from side to side as they created whatever it was emerging on the empty white page of their sketch book. Jimmy must have been working fast. Tyler heard him flip a page and keep right on drawing. He considered inquiring but decided against it for two reasons. He was enjoying the quiet, and enjoying the notion that they were so engrossed in their creative process. He remembered times like that when Momma would pass through the room without saying a word as he was busy in his own world of imagination. One out-of-place word can derail the dream of things to come that inspire such moments in a child's life. And it must be said in adults as well, if they will allow their imagination a freedom from practical worries.

Sometimes the boys would finish something and come present it to their daddy. Just as often they kept it, it seemed to Tyler, as some kind of almost-private journal of their mind. They would never have been angry at their dad had he picked up their books and looked through them, but he was always inclined to let them decide when they wanted him to look. This, to his mind, was a kind of unspoken lesson in boundaries. He knew of friends growing up whose parents never afforded any level of trust to their children. There was no concept of privacy, and with it was lost virtually any sense of imagination and creativity. At least that's what it looked like to Tyler in his far freer world with Momma and Pappy.

An hour and a half into the trip Johnny suggested, "We could eat anytime."

His timing was good. Tyler had just seen a sign for Cracker Barrel, next exit.

Tyler set the expectation for the stop. "This is a breakfast stop only. We are not buying a bunch of candy to all get sick on in the car. So walk right through their store without big eyes on Milk Duds or M & M's. Got it? After all, Jesus said don't take anything extra, according to Jimmy."

"Way to go, Jimmy," was Johnny's reply.

After the feast the afternoon before, it was surprising any of them were hungry, but they'd skipped eating anything after they got home from the park. Now they all ordered big breakfasts with biscuits, gravy, apples, bacon, eggs and grits. Whatever Jimmy might not finish, the other two would. They were all three focused on two things. Eating and getting back on the road. Tyler looked around at the other tables. Table after table on their smart phones. Food getting cold or half wasted. Not talking to each other. He didn't say anything to the boys, but he was so thankful in that moment that they never looked at others with any sense they were somehow missing out. Tyler was sure the three of them were among the few seated there that morning who were *not* missing out.

Tyler said, "You've hauled everything off those plates. Are you two harvest ants ready to go?"

Each made a quick pit stop and Tyler pulled in next door to top up the tank and get a large coffee. He had a small cooler in the front seat stocked with orange La Croix drinks which both boys liked, so he had them already taken care of.

"Boys, I think I over carb'ed at breakfast. I could take a nap with no problem. Hopefully, the extra coffee will keep me awake." The idea of naps at their age seemed like an old-man problem. They certainly weren't sleepy; quite the contrary. "Johnny, why don't you read some of your new book to Jimmy and me—*What Color Is My World?*"

Johnny reached across the back seat to get his backpack, put his sketch book in and took out the book. He thumbed through it for a bit and started in. Between the stories of the different inventors, they would take a break to talk about them and stare out at the passing landscape. Then Johnny would take a sip of his La Croix and start the next story.

Once during a pause, Jimmy asked, "Daddy, did you ever invent anything?"

Tyler said, "I sure did, though I can't claim full credit. Like some of these inventors there was collaboration."

"What did you invent?" Jimmy asked.

"Two very inquisitive boys."

Johnny corrected Tyler. "God did that. He just gave 'em to you so we wouldn't bother him for every little thing. That's what dads are for."

Tyler said, "By golly, I stand corrected. I think you're right!"

All three were really enjoying the book and Johnny said, "Momma and Pappy would like how Mr. Mital sees history all around him. He's a lot like you, Daddy, for seein' things we ought to know about."

"High praise—gratefully accepted. Keep on if you're up to it," Tyler replied.

Johnny said, "How about Jimmy takin' a turn?"

Tyler said, "Jimmy let's hear you read the next story." Jimmy wasn't up to Johnny's reading level but readin' aheada one's grade ran in the family. Tyler could tell he substituted a word here and there when he wasn't too sure how to pronounce it, but replaced it with what he thought would do and still keep to the story. Certainly a few times he made for new expressions that diverted a bit from the author's intent, but not so as to ruin the tellin'. Both boys read expressively. With Jimmy's reading, you just had to enjoy the creative editing that went with it.

As they got deep into the mountains closer to Boone, all reading and drawing were set aside. They were excited about getting close to their new home. The boys took turns laying out what they thought their summer would be like, and Tyler shared with them his notions of what his first weeks at a new job would be like.

Tyler knew one big change was the lack of a support structure that was inherent in the neighborhood back in Macon. He had all his relatives and plenty of good neighbors to call on if he needed any help with the boys. Now, he'd be on his own to sort something out. Landing in Boone in the summer meant weekdays of boys at home. They didn't really need a babysitter, but he thought they needed some type of observation at some level. He certainly wasn't going to ask "Mr. August" to assume such a role.

I had been wondering about this myself. If he did want some regular person coming over for at least part of a day, what would I suggest? I came up empty every time. I did have one idea that I turned around in my mind for several days. Was it possible I was going to suggest this wild notion to Tyler? August Kibler—the small-child avoider? I decided when they arrived I would, with the careful understanding that this was something I and they could try out. No long-term guarantees.

When the Jemison boys pulled up, I was out to greet them by the time they got out of their vehicle. I welcomed the newest residents of Boone and shook each's hand. Tyler gave himself a good middle-age stretch trying to work out a few hundred miles of kinks. Before going into the apartment he pulled up the door of the U-Haul. I took one look and said, "You boys did pack light."

They arrived on Wednesday. Tyler wanted to try to get his driver's license on Thursday or Friday at the latest. He would get as much done before starting work as possible. After the license, then registration and car insurance, and hopefully line up someone who could serve as someone to call if the boys needed something and couldn't get ahold of him at work. Neither had ever made a habit of calling him when he was working, and the times Ruby or Claudine had to help out since Momma Daisy was gone were few and far between.

There was nothing in the load that required my assistance, so I let them get on with it and told Tyler to come see me for a minute when they got unloaded.

He knocked on the door and I hollered, "Come on in." I wasn't sure whether to expect the boys to be with him or not. I rather hoped not.

Tyler said, "The boys are checking out that new TV. The only other one they ever saw that big was at my cousin Dewayne's. That was quite a surprise."

I replied, "Well, I thought the only thing over there that looked like a hunk-a-junk was that old relic. I'm rather glad you came alone, because it's the boys I wanted to talk about. Now, I know before today we've met all of three times and never for more than an hour. Two or three hours isn't long to get to know someone, but just the same, I want to make an offer to you. It comes in two options. It occurred to me that your boys probably don't need round the clock supervision when you're at work. But it also occurred to me, you'd be worrying about them in a new place with no one they know anywhere near. So, option one is, I'm here—if they need to knock my door for anything, they should feel free to do so. Also, you can call me anytime if you need me to do something for them or for you, and if I'm going to be out of pocket or out of town for some reason, I'll let you know ahead of time. How does that sound?"

Tyler was clearly surprised. "Firstly, it's offering a lot, and it sounded to me like option two ran into option one somewhere there with your offer to do for me or the boys if something was needed."

"No," I said, "That was all option one. Option two is option one plus during these summer months, the boys could have breakfast over here on Mondays and go with me to the Daisy Cafe the rest of the week when you're working."

"Lord, have mercy, Mr. August. Did you lose your mind between our first trip to Boone and now? I can't imagine that is something you'd want to take on Monday to Friday."

I answered, "The doctor, if I'd ever go to one, would still at this point declare me of sound mind."

Tyler inquired, "You don't ever go to the doctor? Now, you sound like Momma Daisy. Pappy would go. She never would."

I said, "I knew I liked that woman. Miles went to the doctor all the time and he's dead. I never go, and I'm still here."

He smiled and said, "Now you really sound like Momma!"

"I'll reassure you that I would take the boys to one if the need arose."

Tyler said, "Option two sounds pretty good. You can always opt out if you change your mind."

Moving between my bilingual proper English and my dialect English I said, "Well, then it's dun-did. Monday morning, Operation Jemison Boys goes into action."

Tyler shook my hand and said, "You have no idea the worry you just lifted from my shoulders. I thought, how am I going to start a new job and not be frettin' about those boys being home alone all summer?"

I added my two cents, "And I thought, if Momma Daisy were here she'd be tellin' me, 'Old man, the other side of that booth down there at the Daisy Cafe don't need to be sittin' empty when there's two hungry boys could be blessin' your life.'"

Laughing at the thought of that Tyler said, "If Momma Daisy set this up, then there ain't no way but forward."

Chapter Nineteen

I had invited my new neighbors over for my special-recipe pecan waffles on Saturday, and Tyler accepted. When we were done eating, the boys went in the backyard to explore. Tyler and I sat down with another cup of coffee at the kitchen table looking out to the yard. Penny-girl went out her dog door as was her habit after any meal. Normally, she was very shy around people. Miles, Bonnie and I were her pack and no others were to be trusted. Sometimes I thought, perhaps in this regard, she had the best instincts for people, much better than her so-called masters, and no comparison to our goldens who would befriend anyone and everyone for life. Imagine my surprise when I saw her following them around the yard. Jimmy reached down to pet her and, while a little shy, she didn't do her usual full-retreat when someone would approach her. Next thing, he was laying on the grass petting her. Even Penny-girl was embracing the new presence of these boys. Perhaps she was thinking our pack was thinning out and needed some new blood.

It wasn't long before the boys discovered the graveyard, which they studied for some time before both were in the swing next to it. That occupied them a while, as did sitting on the fountain and lightly splashing each other.

I hadn't discussed my occupation with Tyler, but it did occur to me it might be useful to do so as he began his new job. I told Tyler of the three positions I'd held at the university.

"When I was first hired, I came in as the assistant director of the physical plant and was responsible for overseeing all construction projects. I had the good fortune of coming in after a very able and humble man who had built excellent relationships on campus and off. He was retiring, and fortunately, I was able to shadow him for two weeks before he left for good. The director's instructions on my first day were simple enough. 'Don't screw it up.'

"When the director retired, I moved into that job quite reluctantly. As far as I was concerned, I had one of the best jobs on campus. I have always loved construction and, as hard as it is to believe, I even liked most construction workers. I don't have to tell you there are great exceptions to the rule—those who never met a corner they didn't like to cut—but most knew this was their lifetime vocation and wanted to see a job well done as much as I did. It certainly helped that my predecessor had maintained a list in his office, and passed on to me those who had burned him in the past.

"By the time the director retired, we had a relatively new CFO, Sadie LaMotte. "Dr. Sadie" and I got to know each other quite quickly, in part due to her own genuine interest in construction. Her father had built custom homes, and she loved learning from him—actually working on his crew in the summer months in later high school years and college. We both had high trust in the other. She actually had a new strategy for the organization of her division which she wanted to roll out over the course of the next couple years. She added, 'It wouldn't do your retirement any harm either.' She knew going in that I intended to retire earlier than most. I took the job and passed off most of my responsibilities to a youngster I had been mentoring, who I hoped would step into my job when I retired. He just got the job a little ahead of schedule, though I didn't sense he minded that. A couple years later, she had her new structure in place, and I was now the associate vice president of finance and operations, charged with overseeing the physical plant as well as all other contracted and auxiliary services. I had a small but competent team of directors overseeing the various aspects of my part of the organization. The physical plant, which had long had a director and three assistant directors, now had two directors. My mentored young man moved into one of the director positions still in charge of construction and now directly over the trades as well—always was a more logical fit."

I then noted the key difference between my situation and Tyler's, "You are not going to have the luxury of coming in after a very able and humble city manager. You, my boy, are going directly into the shithole and have to find your way out. Given my time here, I've gotten to know a lot of people in the city, as well as contractors, good and bad, and most of the muckety-mucks in town. If I can ever steer you towards some help in a situation, or away from the snares of the devil, you let me know. For that matter, any help I could give in deciding which might be which," adding, "You've got to watch those tricky snakes. They might look harmless, and the first thing you know they've sunk their fangs right into you."

Tyler responded, "Indeed, that kind of experience with the lay of the land here might be very helpful, and there certainly are similarities in our jobs. After all, the university is kind of a city within a city."

I then added, "Also, I know it might feel a little tricky with John since he is head of city council, but as far as integrity and discretion go, I'm confident you will see the same John Cross I've known all these years. You can take what he says to the bank. I wouldn't be shy about letting him know if you see anything that concerns you, or wonder if you should say something or not. I personally would err on the side of letting him know. I can't extend that to the Mayor or other council members. I don't know any of them well enough to know if they are foxes in lambs' clothing or not. There again, John would know."

"From my brief time with him, that certainly was my first impression," Tyler said. "I'm glad you can confirm it."

I wrapped up our work-talk with, "You get the joy of the public, and I had the joy of academics. I'm not sure who comes out ahead in that."

Tyler laughed and said, "I suspect it's a toss-up."

The boys came back from their exploration of the backyard. "Is everything in order out there?" I asked.

It was obvious they had something on their minds, but seemed a bit afraid to ask. I said, "Out with it. You can ask me anything."

Johnny got his nerve and said, "We saw a headstone with a man's name. Is he buried back there with all the dogs?"

"Sorta," I said. "Do you know what cremation is?"

Jimmy said, "Aunt Claudine's church has sumin' where they put ashes of dead people. Is that what you mean?"

"That is exactly what I mean. That man lived here in this house with me for almost thirty years, and we knew each other all the way back to when we were both in college."

Johnny looked at his daddy now. "Is this the same as cousin Jo Carol and Tracy?"

I think Tyler was getting a little nervous about prying into my personal life and was looking for a diplomatic intervention. He answered him saying, "I don't know Johnny. You know Jo Carol and Tracy are married. Maybe Mr. August and the other gentleman were long-time friends or partners."

"Jimmy jumped in long enough to say, "Mr. Miles was his first name. I couldn't reckon the last name. I'd never seen it before."

"Boys, Miles last name was Bergeron. It looks like that would be pronounced burg - er -on, but the 'g' is said as a 'j' and the 'n' at the end is just kinda dropped. And yes, when the law allowed, we married."

Jimmy asked, "Momma Daisy died in her rockin' chair. Did Mr. Miles die here?"

Tyler jumped in and said, "Mr. August might not want to talk about that right now."

I put him at ease, "I don't mind. A lot of people act like talkin' about the dead is something to avoid, but I remember from our first breakfast at the Daisy Cafe when I asked about your grandmother, Johnny said, 'That'n dead.' Miles died peacefully in the back bedroom. He died with prayer beads in his hand. He said prayers every morning before he got up. I would show you the kind of beads I'm talkin' about, but they are buried under that headstone. They are called the rosary."

Jimmy made a connection to their own family. "Momma Daisy buried our grandpa Horatio's dog tag under his headstone."

"Boys, we do those things for us to sorta move on," I said. "It's parta how they will live on in our hearts. When we see someone's dog tags or a rosary or a rocking chair, our memories come bubblin' up. Sometimes that may make us sad or lonely, but it's been my experience that it's far more likely to bring joy and gratitude. You can't feel sorry for yourself when you know you've been loved all your life. You know all about those feelin's and that love from your Momma Daisy and Pappy, don't you?"

Tyler sighed, "Do we ever. Boys we need to git, and let this man have some peace."

I went straight to my computer and sent Tyler an email. I was a bit concerned that the dying, cremation and headstone account might have been a little over the top for my new neighbor's boys. Later that day came the reply.

Not at all. They are curious boys, and when they ask questions I try to give them as much as I think they can take in. You done good. Your friend, Tyler

Operation Jemison Boys went off without a hitch. The boys quickly settled into the routine and would crack the door open on Monday mornings with Johnny always hollering in, "Anybody home?" And I'd always respond, "Come on in." On the Daisy Cafe mornings, I would knock at their door and I would hear inside, "Comin!"

Down at the cafe, the boys settled into the same seats in the booth across from me—Jimmy always by the wall. I noticed both boys were left-handed, and I was quite sure Tyler was right-handed. A trait from their mother perhaps. When we'd get there, Noel would tell them about once a week, "I hope you two checked that old man's wallet to be sure he's got some money; otherwise you two are going to be back here washin' dishes."

Johnny in response would say, "We checked. He's loaded!"

Soon after Noel had first arrived to run the cafe, I gave him two recipes from my mother. One was for cinnamon rolls and the other was for her mincemeat. He added mincemeat pie as a regular addition to the menu, and the cinnamon rolls he would offer only on Fridays, Saturdays and Sundays. The boys told me about Aunt Claudine's garden, and how bartering led to them having mincemeat pie at Thanksgiving and Christmas. I told them I'd never been in any restaurant that served it and convinced Noel that offering something off the beaten track might prove popular, which it did with a few loyal customers.

While I stuck to my usual breakfasts, the boys would change things up from one day to the next. They brought one orange La Croix drink with them each time to share, and would have eggs, bacon or sausage one day, or oat meal and toast, or biscuits and gravy. Friday was the exception. Every Friday that summer they would have a cinnamon roll and two pieces of bacon. There was a time when I would have had one as well. I made my mother's rolls many times going back to my college days, when I would even bake up enough to share with the entire choir. I was a big hit at many gatherings since I would come carrying two or three pans, fresh out of the oven. Sadly, as age advanced, so did my tonnage. By the time I reached 250 pounds I was beginning to face a lot of chronic ailments. Among the first things to go were those cinnamon rolls and mincemeat pies. My "healthy eating" phase didn't improve my aches and pains, which were only getting worse. I lost about twenty pounds, but by my legs alone I could see that was all muscle mass I was giving up. Miles was even worse off than me. His doctor had him on too many meds and with every passing year seemed to add at least on more pill or injection. After Miles died, I took a different tack when Ethel's doctor suggested we read *The New Adkins*. My chronic ailments were gone within six months, and I finally was gaining and not losing muscle mass. Still, cinnamon rolls remained my personal casualty to my new lifestyle choice.

Ethel told the boys those were my mother's recipe, and I told the boys, "Enjoy them now, but know one day you might have to give up such foods. Never get locked into thinking you can eat anything you want. Your body will not respond well, though it may take it years to protest in earnest."

While we were enjoying ourselves at the Daisy Cafe, poor Tyler learned just what fun it was to land in a shithole. John Cross took as much time as he could manage from his own business to offer Tyler all the help possible. The Mayor was good to work with, but not nearly as helpful to the problems that had to be overcome as John. Tyler knew if he was stuck at work, I'd do what needed to be done to see to the boys. He always left them with some simple makings for lunch, but tried to be home to cook dinner or take the boys out. When he couldn't, I did one or the other. If we went out, we always dropped something off for Tyler on our way home.

They had no sooner landed in Boone than his Aunt Ruby emailed Tyler saying that she and Uncle Ira wanted to see if it would be all right for them to come up and spend some time with the boys. They knew he'd be too busy to spend any time with them and not to feel like he needed to. They hoped it might help him out a bit over the summer. They would stay in a hotel and come over to the house during the days as well as take the boys over to the hotel pool. Tyler noticed that their dates happened to overlap the 4th of July. He knew that was no coincidence. He also had sense enough to thank them for the offer and that he looked forward to seeing them real soon.

I was looking forward to meeting Ira and Ruby. Tyler had told me about their timber frame workshop, and remodeling of the house, and all the way back to their industrial arts class. I told Tyler, "You're tellin' the story like your Momma Daisy—workin' your way backwards."

He laughed, "I hadn't even thought about that!"

Tyler brought the two of them over to my apartment.

"Come in! Come in," as I motioned them through the door. "Now, I've heard all about your timber frame master work you two crafted together. I don't need you lookin' too close at my poor factory-made version. And you'll see I didn't have a Ruby to make me any beautiful stained glass windows."

Ira said, "We inspected Tyler's side pretty closely. It looks to us like there is at least one timber framer in North Carolina who knows how to craft beauty into a building. And you, Mr. August, have certainly made them a home."

I responded, "Knowing what I know of the Jemisons, that is high praise, gratefully acknowledged."

I started a fresh pot of coffee, and we all strolled into the backyard. As all are, they were drawn back to the cemetery. It appeared that Tyler had already spelled out the one human headstone amongst the dogs' stones. They strolled silently around the yard and then settled into the chairs on the patio. I arrived with the coffee and fixin's if anything was needed in their coffee, and we settled in for a nice visit. Of course, Billy had come with them to North Carolina. He was over with the boys next door. Working our way backward, as was the Jemison custom, they talked about their new life with the boy. I asked, "Does he seem to miss his brothers and sisters or Vivian? I suspect he doesn't miss Joab from what I've heard about him from Tyler."

Ruby said, "I think he's trying to forget Joab and his siblings as quickly as possible. Vivian has called a couple times to talk to him on the phone since she dropped him off. Of course, that was pretty recent—just as Tyler was leaving Macon. We plan to adopt the boy if they will sign off, which we're sure Joab will do without a second thought."

Ira made a long, loud sigh, "Ah, that child o' ours and her family caused Momma and Daddy a lot of grief. Momma said once to me, 'Grieving your brother dying in that useless war was one kind of grief, but all the love remained. With Vivian and that Washington mess, I grieve as though there is no amount of light that can overturn their darkness.' Ruby and I know exactly how that feels. Now we've got this boy that was the only light in that house, and he's found his way to us. It may sound a bit old fashioned to say it, but if that ain't Momma's and Daddy's doing from the other side of life, I ain't sure how it ever come to be."

"Ira," I said, "I have never had to deal with the kind of wound that is inflicted by a child who just seems to move from one bad choice to the next, as they descend deeper and deeper into the dark. Jesus said we were to make heaven here on earth and, with all the beauty and wonder of this earth, I don't understand how some can look past it all. It is so beautiful. I'll admit, I'm not really worried if I live for an eternity in some other life after this one. It seems to me we're called to live in this life. The rest will take care of itself. And in those times when I feel all my doubts bubble up, something comes along renewing the mystery of it all, alive again in my mind. Sometimes that happens when I look back and have to wonder what was leading me when I didn't feel led. Sometimes it happens, as it has these past couple months, when a certain Momma Daisy and Pappy seem to be working things out for Tyler, Johnny, Jimmy and Billy."

Ruby added rather matter-of-factly, "All we can say to the doubters is, 'Make of that what you will.'"

The 4th came and went without a flag flying at either apartment. There was a time when Miles and I would have put out a big flag on the porch. We both became so weary of the hubris that was laid bare with all the violence we inflicted as a country on the rest of the world and on ourselves, that the flag meant nothing to us anymore. This was fueled in no small part by the flags lined up one after another whenever our presidents are on the stage selling their latest lie. I very unceremoniously put ours in the trash. We kept our views to ourselves mostly, but I soon enough learned that the Jemisons' own journey through what it means to love one's country brought them to much the same place. I knew too that, for the Jemisons, this day in particular was a day of remembrance, and I was sure to treat it as such.

Uncle Ira barbecued a brisket and some chicken, Ruby and Tyler made some side dishes, and I was invited to join them. I offered to bring whatever might be wanted but was told to just bring myself, so I did. I had seen Billy, but hadn't been around him yet to that point. The boy was an angel—in looks and disposition. All I could think of was how remarkable it was that the child would be able to skip an entire generation of terrible, and land himself back to the folk who knew how to love. It also made me incredibly sad at the thought of all those boys and girls who are in homes like the Washington mess, without any place to escape. I wondered how many generations of Washingtons there were before Joab, and now the six other victims that he and Vivian had following in their wake, where hate and cruelty were as natural to them as taking a shit. I kept such thoughts to myself on this occasion. With such turning over in my mind I was tuning out the world around me. Finally, I re-awakened to the day and to the playful joy of the three boys to bring me out of my temporary funk. The smell of the barbecue would just as quickly bring me back to the best of "making table" as the old Mennonites would say—with friends and family, where even the dead have a place at the table as they flood our hearts and minds with their presence. Such was this day for me, and every bit more so for the Jemisons, who would mark this day of remembrance for Horatio Spafford Jemison….blown to bits by the hubris and greed of men and the futility of war. Yes, if there is one day where this old man finds it hard to keep the funk at bay, it is this day, the 4th of July.

Chapter Twenty

Over the summer, Tyler had continued to barbecue on Sundays, and I was always invited and always accepted. It was perhaps a payment in his mind for my breakfasts during the week with the boys. Fortunately, neither of us viewed the gifts of hospitality as any debt being accrued. We were in some way family now, and the only thing that really mattered was being grateful for all that we had to be grateful for.

I couldn't help but notice that no Sunday morning church interfered with Sunday plans, and Tyler had never asked me about churches in the area which I thought he might. A good evangelical would have been on them by now to get involved, but if I learned anything about church over the years, it was that beating someone over the head with your religion doesn't bring peace to the world or the soul. Besides, Johnny let me know the first Sunday after Ira, Ruby and Billy went back to Macon, "Right now, we's barbecue Baptist."

I told Tyler on the sly, "That would have to be the best kinda Baptists I've run across yet."

Fortunately for Tyler, Sundays were as light as it got for city manager business. He would get a call which might string into two or three follow-up calls or a conference call, but he could almost always deal with it from home. His demeanor on the calls, whatever was happening, suggested he was able to handle what came his way—keeping his stride and talking others off the ledge as the need arose.

They always gave me a doggie bag, literally—meat scraps for Penny-girl who would chomp it down as though she hadn't eaten in a week. In her old age she was getting pickier. Her favorite remained liver—chicken or calve's, but any meat would do. Dog food mostly sat in the bowl, except what I would mix in with her preferred fare. Even then, she would eat around most of that and eat it only when all the meat pieces were gone from her plate. Her now mostly carnivore diet kept her going, as well as one could expect of an old mid-size dog. She wobbles a lot more these days and occasionally falls, but unfazed she takes a minute to regain her balance and goes on her way. I'm prepared for whatever comes. For now, she keeps me grounded at home and that's just fine.

The summer went by quickly. The boys got their new bikes when Ruby, Ira and Billy had gone back to Macon. Tyler didn't want to make Billy feel left out with the two boys having new bikes. Both boys reminded me of the hours I'd spent going up and down our quiet country road. I loved riding bike. I would pedal as fast as possible down our gravel road. I never took any real bad spills, though I did scrape a palm now and then. In those days, we weren't nearly so careful as proper bike safety calls for these days. It's good to see the protective equipment to make sure a simple spill doesn't turn into a serious injury. I certainly observed over the years something one of my uncles said to me once, "Young people don't see danger." Looking back at my childhood and observing the young ever since, I'd go so far as to say that is so true, and perhaps even understated.

At least until next summer, Operation Jemison Boys would be shut down. The boys were experiencing their first week in a new school. While the weather permitted they would ride their bikes to school. Tyler reminded them of something they already knew from their Macon school days. If other kids laughed at a classmate for not being able to read as well or add as well as the others, they were not only to not join in, but should try to befriend the boy or girl who the others in the class were belittling.

The Jemisons had enough Momma and Pappy in them not to get their feelings hurt easily if someone tried to pick on them. Both boys would be ahead of most of their classmates and knew it wasn't theirs to lord over anyone. So it was not surprising that at the first parent-teacher conference, both boys' teachers had nothing but praise for them boys. They had settled in and seemed to enjoy school far more than I ever did.

I'm delighted there are those who like school—even love it. I mostly hated it. College was a little better, but there too, it couldn't end soon enough to suit me. I would see to it I graduated, but in all my years of high school and college the honor roll and dean's list would elude me. More accurately, I would elude them. I actually did make the dean's list the first semester of my freshman year. I'd had an older brother who flunked out his first term. I was determined not to follow in his footsteps, so I studied like crazy that first semester. Once I realized I could get by with less effort, I slid into my high school pattern of trusting my wits to get me by more than my discipline.

In full disclosure I also worked twenty to thirty hours a week — sometimes more. The luxury of being a full-time student with parents picking up the tab was not something I ever was afforded. From high school through graduate school I worked. There were times in college I was just struggling to stay awake in another boring lecture. My tiredness didn't come from partying too much — it was from work.

It took me a lot of years to sort though my learning proclivities. It wasn't that I didn't want to learn, but the standard lecture and standard textbook were not my idea of inspirational instruction. Yet that prevailed in all the instruction I received, with only a couple exceptions from a couple of exceptional "educators." I learned from observation and doing. If most don't learn that way, I'd like to see the evidence to the contrary. Somewhere along the line, imagination got pushed aside in favor of conformity. And conformity and growth don't exist in a symbiotic relationship. The beech forest may, at an unstudied glance, appear to exist in a nature of great conformity, but every seedling must find its way into the soil, absorb the water and nutrients, and reach towards the sunlight. They twist and turn and stretch their branches toward life. They toil, not in some perceived need of conformity to the trees around them. Their diversity brings with it the contemplative beauty of timeless freedom and the forces that acted upon their time. They will drop their leaves each season and their branches in years until one day, the last remaining life is returned to humus for the cycle to begin again.

One of the exceptional teachers I had was also rather eccentric — a trait I would appreciate in several others in time — and looking back, a non-conformist as well. He taught the only Old Testament class I would ever take, and instead of boring lectures on how the Church of God interpreted these ancients books, or dates to memorize, he poured out all the imagination hidden in them along with the absurdity of trying to formulate them into one set of beliefs. He used a textbook of sorts by W. W. Sloan—one that remains on my bookshelf, but one that, in reflection years later, mirrored more his weaving of a narrative than presenting the dry timelines and "facts" that some typical history book would normally offer. My New Testament professor was far more popular, God knoweth why, than my eccentric OT professor, and that next semester returned me to mental oblivion in his droning lectures and memorization-required exams. I would get an A in OT and squeak out a C in NT.

Over the years, I've read a lot of books. And wonder of wonders, never have I gone out and bought a textbook, and never have I seen textbooks on people's home library shelves. Shouldn't that suggest something about life-long learning? I am a great believer in mentorship, apprenticeship, stewardship. These I believe are foundational to passing along skills, patience and wisdom to those wanting to learn. I see little reason most "instruction" can't be built on the strength of each of these. You might say I'm for a lot of "ships" and few or no "isms." Fundamentalism, socialism, communism, capitalism, liberalism, conservatism. It seems to me, people can take anything with possible merit and turn it into an ism to the exclusion of all else, while extolling their pride in having done so. I could find something to ponder as a good from each of these isms and yet, as understood in our culture, I can't affix my devotion to any one of them. As Ruby said, make of that what you will. It seems increasingly apparent that even education latches onto the agenda of these isms, as certainly the media does, and we end up with a lot of angry, cynical and it must be said, dumb people educated right into stupidity. Humility will open our eyes to our own ignorance, but the pride that prevails only ensures passing along stupidity from one generation to the next.

One Sunday afternoon Tyler brought up the matter of church. He approached me saying, "Soon it will be getting too cold to continue to be barbecue Baptists. I didn't want to sacrifice the hours I had these first weeks here with the boys sitting in church. Momma would have understood that, but she'd probably be thinkin' about now, I ought to be doing something about gettin' these boys in church. Any suggestions? I know you talked 'Episcopalian' with Uncle Ira and Aunt Ruby."

I started by saying, "I've been afraid you'd ask me that question. I have a complicated love-hate relationship with Christianity. Music and liturgy kept Miles and me engaged a lot longer than we would have ever otherwise been. You won't find it surprising that two men don't feel welcome in more churches than not and that, even where you think you're welcome, you find out over time the welcome was anything but universally held no matter how active you were in the church.

"When I first got to Baton Rouge, I commented to an acquaintance—who thought we'd lost our way when we left the Church of God to go to the Episcopal church—that having been Mennonite, Church of God and now attending the Episcopal church, it appeared to me they all preached the same Gospel. At one level I'd still say that's true, but I'd add as well, that I've learned too much about the blind complicity to empire that they live by the rest of the week. They quote from the Gospels but it appears it costs them little to do so. As the trustees of the diocese once said to me when I called them out on a few rather ethically and morally troublesome companies in their endowment funds, 'We have a fiduciary responsibility to uphold.' That the bishop sat there and said nothing was most disconcerting. It wasn't just another straw on my back. They had hoisted a bale upon it, which I would be unwilling to carry for much longer."

I then asked, "You're divorced, I presume?" This was my first time to bring this subject up.

Tyler said, "The boys' mother lives in Panama, where she left us to live for reasons never made fully clear. That was several years ago. Jimmy's only memory of her is from a picture of her with the boys I kept on the mantle in the living room. I still have the picture, but it's packed away, and I wondered if they'd ask about it. They haven't yet. Officially, we divorced in June."

I revealed the reason for the question at this time, "If you plan to remarry, there are worse places to meet a spouse than at church. Miles' brothers like to troll bars in search of companionship. It never seemed to Miles or me that the bar net was catching anything one would want to keep, and as the years passed they were forever throwing them back after a few years of marriage. Then they'd go to the same hole where they caught the last one and fish again."

Tyler added, "The classic sign of insanity—doing the same thing over and over expecting a different result."

"Exactly," I said. "These days more are fishin' online. I suppose that's a way and maybe a step-up from the bars, assuming some due diligence is given to the process, but I don't know why I'm going on about all that. You may not want to get married. You may just want a church for the boys to feel part of something bigger. I certainly can understand that."

Tyler proceeded, "Well, for the record I would consider marrying again, and you'll be glad to know, but probably not surprised to hear, that I wouldn't plan to go fishin' in the bars. For every couple I know who met online and are on to their way to happily-ever-after, three others were pretty much a disaster in no time. Of course, marriage, disaster and dysfunction seem to abound, and what I know of the Old Testament, this is not a new phenomenon."

I agreed, "Indeed it is not. I've told a lot of Christian mothers carrying guilt over their imperfect families to go study the Bible and find where a happy, functional family ever existed."

"I would like the boys to be part of something, I guess," Tyler continued. "Momma felt like the church was movin' away from her, and you seem to be saying the same thing in some ways. I don't expect perfection, but so much of art and music has had its expression in the message of the scriptures, that it seems a shame to deprive the boys of being part of that."

I agreed, "Well said, young man. With your ecumenical family, you know the options about as well as I do. For simpler church polity, congregational churches have something to recommend them. Of course, you can't predict what that local congregation is going to be like until you step through the door. They could be from one end of the spectrum to the other. For liturgy, both the Lutherans and Episcopalians have something to recommend them. In my limited experience, with the Lutherans you get better singing and with the Episcopalians generally a better pipe organ. Of course the Lutherans have their factions. I don't see you as fitting too well with the Missouri bunch.   Catholics, Methodists, Baptists, Church of Christ—they all conjure up an image which might vary a bit from one church to the next, but aren't radically different from what you would conjure up. Mega churches are all the craze, and for certitude, would be hard to beat. Most definitely not my cup of tea. I'd rather have my doubts and be wrong than to be certainly wrong.   I don't think you'll find any Mennonites or Quakers around here.   I guess those are out by default.   My own ideal would be Quaker polity with Anglican music which doesn't seem to exist. You might find some good music in some black churches, but I have no idea what to suggest there."

Tyler said, "At this point I'm leaning towards the Episcopal Church.   The times we went there with Uncle James and Aunt Claudine—and of course, Pappy's and Momma's funerals were there—I really liked it, and the boys seemed pretty intrigued with it. I'm not sure if they have much going for kids though."

"A mystery of our time," I said. "The biggest churches get the most kids teaching them all manner of things which would be better left untaught."

"That's my fear of joining the wrong church," Tyler said.

"Tyler, you have one benefit a good many parents don't. Your boys make their own entertainment and enjoy, as much as any kids ever, being part of the grown-up world. They are tuned into adult conversations like few I've ever seen.   In that regard, I guess I'd suggest driving out to Valle Crucis. There is a small church there. I don't think it has any kids, at least of any regular presence, but I gather it's a rather special place. The roof won't fall in if you give it a try. If I ever try again with the church, I'll probably try it. It's a beautiful church in a beautiful setting. I did go there once soon after Miles died. If I do go, I'll just have to tune a few things out at this stage of my life."

Chapter Twenty-one

The next Sunday, the barbecue-Baptists decided to take the drive out to Valle Crucis to check it out. Jimmy and Johnny wanted to know if I should be invited since we did spend Sundays together. Tyler said, "Don't go over and ask him. Just call him on the phone. It will be easier that way if he wants to say no."

When they called I said, "Well, I'll go to be sure y'all can find the place." I thought that left me open to not make it a habit. My second visit and their first confirmed two things. It is a special place and no kids were in sight. The youngest person there was a young man who appeared to be college age—probably attending the university as he was not there with anyone else. I wondered if Tyler did the same math as I. With the young man it made for 10% black, 90% white in attendance.

Our pew did some pretty good singing, and we had more than a few invitations back to the parish hall. Tyler looked to me to decide.

I said, "It's up to you. You'll get a feel for their hospitality if you do."

I've been in such after-service social times when the visitor is welcomed from the sanctuary only to find no one makes any attempt to talk to them when they are back drinking coffee. Everyone goes into their little habitual cliques. The stranger is left off on the side to sip coffee by his or herself. That was not the case here. More than one recognized Tyler as the new city manager, though that didn't seem to be what inspired their hospitality. They seemed both generous and genuine. We ended up staying until the group started to wind down. Both the rector and curate and a dozen others talked to Tyler and me and Johnny and Jimmy, treating them like the mature boys they were.

When we got in the car to head back to Boone, Jimmy said, "Them people is real nice."

Johnny said, "Where we gonna eat? We could go to the Daisy Cafe."

It's true they hadn't been there since Operation Jemison Boys went into hiatus. "Lord, have mercy," I said. "Ethel and Maggie will certainly be amused if I show up there on a Sunday."

Tyler said, "I was gonna suggest someplace else, but it sounds like it would be worth it for the entertainment value alone."

"Drive on," I said. "The Daisy Cafe it is."

My previous experience with Sundays there was still intact—perhaps even worse. Packed with parents and kids, the volume of which couldn't be cranked up much higher if all tried. Smart phones everywhere. Texting and talking at the same time, I'm sure neither one very coherent—people being the poor multi-taskers they actually are compared to what they think they are. We had to wait about fifteen minutes for a table, but knew on a Sunday we were going to do that most places that are half-decent.

When Ethel got to our table she looked at us and said, "The way you all are dressed, I'd say you just came from church. Did you get this old man into church?"

I answered for them, "Yes, they did, and the roof didn't come down nor trumpets blow from on high."

Picking up where she was headed, "And here you are with your favorite Sunday crowd. Isn't it just the nicest group of families you've ever seen?"

So as to not be too negative in front the boys I said, "Oh, very charming." Then I said, "We'd better have menus. I'm not sure any of us know what Noel cooks other than breakfast."

That wasn't altogether true. There was a time when I had my own lunch trio, and we always flip-flopped between two places—the Daisy Cafe and Indian buffet. After Robert died, Madi and Miles continued to go to lunch just about every day together. They would allow others to join them, but none ever replaced Robert as a permanent addition to their routine, including me.

When my office moved from the physical plant to the main admin building, I got to know better two people I'd known for a long time. Layla was dean of the graduate school and Amelia was director of institutional research. Miles had known them both better than I for a long time, since he was forever producing reports for both offices. Amelia had worked in the office for another director who was one of Miles' least favorite "clients." They would go round and round with Miles, giving him reports straight from the data in the system, and the director insisting it could not be right. He never liked it when an enrollment report looked worse than his forecasts. At one point Miles said to him, "Tell me the numbers you want and I can create a report to match it, but it will only have your name on it and not mine!" The man was close to being certifiable. At one point he screamed at Miles, "I'm ready to blow my damn brains out!" Fortunately, Miles had sense enough to walk away without a word and wait for him to calm down. Amelia had always been the sane voice of reason and worked with the campus, in spite of her boss, to keep somewhat of a good reputation for the office. When the director finally retired, Amelia moved into the office and made it all purr like a kitten.

Layla was really an old peacenik hippy. Most would be clueless of her hippy proclivities. Now, those tie-dye days only appeared on the weekend. She was an Elvis fan and kept a big cardboard cutout in a small storage closet in her office. She'd been in the graduate office for some time and was well-respected as dean. She could navigate around temperamental tenured faculty better than the provost, which was saying something. There were a few who pushed the limits of her commitment to nonviolence— always resolved after work with a good eye rolling and lifting a glass of wine as she'd toast, "May they go far in life and may it be soon!"

When it came to war and peace and justice, all three of us were kindred spirits. While Madi and Miles talked shop, we made every effort to talk about anything but. While it was hard to resist the state of the world, we did our best to not fall victim to outrage fatigue. We were just as likely to share a poem we'd read or written, and talk about music of various genres. We each knew the books the others liked, and when the planets would align, we'd read the same book and report back on our thoughts over lunch at Daisy's or the buffet.

So yes, I actually knew the menu pretty well. In addition to the standard menu, Noel had his daily specials: Tuesday meatloaf; Wednesday Pad Thai; Thursday chicken or beef enchiladas; Friday Flounder; Saturday meat or veggie lasagna; and Sunday pork loin which had a cream cheese, walnut, cranberry stuffing. When Ethel brought the menus, I was glad to see the pork loin was still the

Sunday offering. It was always moist and delicious. I hoped he hadn't run out by now. Fortunately, Ethel said he still had several servings left. I said, "Reserve one for me."

Tyler said, "I'll do that as well."

"I'll let Noel know while the boys decide what they want," and she was off to the kitchen.

Tyler inquired as to their plans, "What are you two thinking about having?"

Jimmy said, "It'd be a shame not to have a cinnamon roll while we're here."

So as to forego possible disappointment I said, "Those are probably long gone by this time of day, but you never know. Looks to me like most of these families ordered tall stacks of pancakes and then left most of it on their plate."

Tyler suggested the roll by itself might not be a meal and pitched to them, "What do you think of splitting the roll with your brother, if they still have one, and sharing the chicken fajitas for two? If you can't eat all the fajitas, I bet I know a little red-heeler that can finish what you don't."

Both boys bought that idea. When Ethel came back I said, "I'll go first. Pork loin, of course, and I'll start with a piece of mincemeat pie."

"Well!" Was all Ethel said. "Coffee?"

"No, I'll stick with water. Thanks, Ethel," I said.

"Boys, you got your mind made up?" she asked.

Johnny took control, "Jimmy and I are gonna share the chicken fajitas for two, and we'll split a cinnamon roll if you still have one. Like Mr. August, we'll take that first."

"Very well," Ethel looked to Tyler and asked, "Cinnamon roll, mince-pie or chocolate cake?"

"I'd better have mince-pie to start out."

Tuesday I was back to my usual booth and routine. Maggie, Ethel and Noel were ribbing me about coming in on a Sunday. Noel said, "I believe those boys could get you to do anything. They'd say jump and you'd say, 'I'm too old, but I'll give it a try.'"

I thought I had a good response to that, "Don't kid yourselves. Those boys could wrap you three around their little fingers just as easily as they do me."

Maggie said, "Tyler needs to give parenting lessons."

I said, "He does, but you gotta have students that are open to learnin'. I didn't see any families in here Sunday that were ready to see that one family stood out as examples to follow. Did you?"

"Point made," she conceded.

She no sooner said that when John Cross came in the cafe. He came over to my booth and sat down. Ethel asked, "You eating or just want coffee?"

"I'll take oatmeal with milk and brown sugar, coffee black, and white toast and butter. Maybe some raisins in the oatmeal if you have 'em."

"We do," Ethel said and was off to get his order. She stopped, realizing she'd not gotten my order yet. "Sausage or Bacon, August?"

"Crispy bacon, please."

"Got it."

I wasn't sure if John was there for a purpose or not. He'd been terribly busy between city work and his own business, but as far as I knew hadn't had any difficulties with Tyler. I hadn't seen him in the cafe since that day in May. I said, "Been a while. How are you doing?"

He answered, "I'm finally getting a chance to get back to some normalcy thanks to Tyler. I understand you told him he'd been dropped in the shithole and would have to find his way out. That was probably good advice, as it certainly dispelled any possible notion that his first weeks were going to be easy."

I was curious, "Are people treatin' him right? Especially those older ones who report to a younger out-of-town whippersnapper?"

John responded, "They saw quick enough he'd get his hands dirty as needs be, and won their respect as quickly as anyone coming in possibly could. He's got a couple that we're gonna have to deal with in some fashion—probably with a boot out the door. I might have already done it, but he's done what's reasonable for them to come around. One was on that course and seems to trying, but he's got two who aren't helping their situations. He's being

147

careful. I can't imagine when they do get their notice of termination that they'd have any legal leg to stand on to sue the city."

I couldn't help but notice that he was talking to me quieter than was his normal voice. He was being sure the ol' boys' table, which was in their own conversation of no importance at the moment, wasn't able to pick up on city employee business. He didn't have to tell me to keep it between us. That was already understood. I'd shared similar tales with some of my staff at the university. I asked him, "So, you think he'll make it out of the shithole?"

John reassured me, "He already has. The young man is doing fine." Then he asked, "Did you hear about the co-conspirator the DA indicted a couple weeks ago?"

I shock my head indicating I had not.

John laid it all out. "In their investigation, they found someone on the payroll who knew what the city manager was doing but never told anyone. He thought he could lie low but, in being questioned as a matter of course, let something slip which told the DA he knew of the embezzlement. The DA pounced on that, knowing it would strengthen his chances with a jury to have his testimony. When the guy seemed reluctant to testify, the DA indicted him as a co-conspirator. That got his attention, but his reluctance also irritated the DA, who then refused to drop the charge. The DA called me yesterday to tell me he'd pleaded out to where all he has to do is six months community service. I told him I hoped he didn't put him at the food pantry; he may load up his trunk for his co-conspirator. The DA said, 'Pickin' up trash along the highway is more what I had in mind.' The DA thinks it will probably end pretty soon without a jury trial. We shall see."

Maggie brought out our breakfasts and filled our coffees. I took one look at that oatmeal with the brown sugar, raisons and toast and said, "That used to be one of my favorite breakfasts. Unlike you, it also helped maintain my gut, which I'm sure you remember well. Enjoy it while you can."

John said, "Don't you know this is healthy?"

I said, "That's what some will tell you anyway. Quaker Oats for one."

Chapter Twenty-two

John Cross, August Kibler and the Jemison family were all finding our stride in our new normal. The school year passed quickly and Operation Jemison Boys resumed. To Tyler's pleasure, John ran for re-election and easily won. He would remain head of the city council. The Mayor was also easily re-elected so Tyler had some confidence that things could continue to plug along without a lot of disruption. They were in the final planning stages of some major projects, which had to be reworked after the last city manager's poor handling of the planning process.

Tyler and the boys visited a few other churches during the school year and also went back to Valle Crucis a couple times. When they'd go there, I'd go along. The rest of their church adventures I skipped and spent quiet Sundays at home with Penny-girl. I began to wonder day to day when her time was going to be up. I could see her get just a little bit weaker and eating just a little less from week to week.

They had some interesting experiences in the churches. In one case Tyler was at an absolute loss as to what to do. He was so upset by the sermon he wanted to walk out. He remembered what I'd said about big churches, with the worst teaching, get the most young families. This was a perfect case in point. He didn't know what the right thing to do was with the boys beside him. Would they be tuned in enough to know what the man was saying? The preacher would have gotten Momma Daisy and Pappy going as much or more than himself. He thought knowing Momma, she wouldn't have walked out. She would have stood up in the middle of it and shut him down. "If you ain't gonna preach the Gospel, you ain't got no business puttin' on the robe, standing in that pulpit preachin' the hate you're preachin'!" That is what he imagined her doing. For sure she'd have left and shaken the dust off her sandals, never to enter again. Tyler opted for the latter response. He literally lightly stomped his feet just outside the door. Not overly dramatic so as not to make it too obvious to the boys. Both of them did the same. He assumed they were just doing as he'd done.

When they got in the car, Johnny said, "It's like Jesus said. We testified agin 'em. Our peace could not rest with them and came to back us."

Jimmy said, "That man was mean! I don't want to go back there."

Tyler might have laughed at their responses, but he was still literally shaken from the experience. "Don't worry about that boys. We'll let the dead bury the dead at that place. It reminds me of a story where a homeless man was sitting on a bench outside a church that wouldn't seat him. Jesus sat down beside him and said, "Don't feel bad. I've been trying to get in there for years."

Most of the other visits were more benign. They'd like the singing at one, the sermon at another. Some were small, poor and clearly needed more membership. Some were easy enough to get lost in the crowd. Some were more integrated than others. Some were not integrated at all.

Tyler also remembered what I'd said about finding someone in a church instead of online or in a bar. He had not resorted to either and still wasn't sure if he even wanted to get involved at this point in their new life. He finally said to me one Sunday afternoon after they'd been to the Lutheran church, "If I'm supposed to meet the love of my life in one of these churches, the prospects thus far are mighty bleak. I don't even know exactly what I'm lookin' for. I just hope I got enough sense to know it when I see it. Jemison men aren't known for being clued into the options out there."

I said, "And yet, Ira Lewis Jemison and Ruby Rose Reed found their way to each other."

Then for the first time he made a bit of a confession. "What if I'm not looking for a Ruby Rose Reed?"

"Humm, well if you're saying what I think you are, then we'll have to just admit the field narrows substantially, and you've got your work cut out for you."

Tyler rather sadly said, "That's what I'm afraid of. I was too scared when I was young, and now I'm coming up on middle-age, and all I see is middle-aged married men. A few, I wonder why they are married, but then so was I."

I thought some of my story might help in some small way. "As you know, Miles and I went all the way back to college.

150

Sophomores to be specific. I couldn't have handled it when I was a freshman. On that famous choir trip I had my epiphany. I was what God had made me and God's grace was sufficient. That is quite literally what went through my mind, laying awake at night, when I faced up to things. The next day I felt like a burden had been lifted from off me. And there was Miles who had already faced up to who he was, and there I was sitting next to him on the bus as we rolled into Macon. And I knew what I had thought before, that I was just envious of him—as I had tried to persuade myself—when in fact I realized, I was in love with him. You shouldn't get discouraged. You're on the hill up towards middle age and have an enormous heart to share. Those are in short supply. And I know this, when you feel like you're not being led, you'll look back and think you were. Maybe it's time for you to say in your prayers, God, I'm ready if you are."

Tyler said, "I think I'm ready to pray that prayer."

Two weeks later, I agreed to ride along since they were going back out for one of their Valle Crucis visits. On the drive out he said, "I'm beginning to feel like we just need to stake a claim somewhere, and it might just as well be Valle Crucis."

I said, "I can imagine they would be delighted to have the Jemisons as regular parishioners."

The couple of times I'd been back with them I had not seen the young college boy. I'd guessed he was just a visitor passing through, but this morning he was back and with him was a somewhat older man. I would have guessed, very close to Tyler's age. I led us to the pew in front of them though that wasn't planned. In fact, I didn't actually notice them until I was started into the pew. When I glanced back I thought to myself, "Momma Daisy, you must want us in this pew. Here I am on the opposite side of where I'd usually go."

With the two voices behind us, we had our own small men's chorus as we all enthusiastically sang the opening hymn—God is working his purpose out as year succeeds to year... I looked over at Tyler. The irony of the hymn was not lost on him either. We both smiled and sang our hearts out. At the peace, we greeted the two behind us. I thought well, if they come to coffee hour, maybe we

151

can find out just what if any purpose is being worked out. The dismissal had barely concluded when Jimmy turned to them and said, "You both sing real nice. Are you coming back to the parish hall?"

Jimmy had asked what I wanted to and refrained from doing.

"Sure," the older one said.

After the customary greetings were exchanged at the door with the clergy, the priest added, "We had quite a baritone section this morning. It's nice to hear people sing like they mean it."

As we all made our way to the parish hall, as senior diplomat I started the introductions. "I'm August Kibler and these are my neighbors and friends, Tyler, Johnny and Jimmy Jemison. The finest young men you could ever meet."

The older one following my lead said, "I'm Christian Marvel and this is my much younger brother, Giles. He's at the university and I was just hired as budget director."

"Well, well," I said, "I know your boss quite well. Dr. Sadie was my boss until I retired, and young Tyler here is Boone city manager." I interceded as best I could at that point, "Boys let's go see what they've got next door," and I took my hands behind two boys' heads and herded them away. I even added, "Giles, you comin' our way?" And he followed, as well, while the other two were left on their own to figure out if they had anything in common besides good jobs in Boone.

I struck up a conversation with Giles. As it turns out, their mother is an Episcopal priest in South Carolina, and their father runs a clock shop which he inherited from his father and back to his grandfather who started it. Giles had one more year before graduating with a degree in environmental biology. I asked, "Is your brother relocating his family here?"

"I'm the only family he'll have for the time being in Boone," he answered. "He isn't married. Yet. I gather he's open to the idea though. And if it's not too shocking to say this these days, he's waiting for the right husband to come along and one hasn't yet."

All I could do is smile and say, "He might need to let God know he's ready if God's ready. And no, I'm not shocked by such a thing. My husband, may he rest in peace, was with me for thirty-five years."

152

"Oh!" Giles said. "I'm sorry to hear he's passed, but I gather you had a good life together."

"Indeed we did."

With a nervous look Giles asked, "Can I be a little nosey? Is there a Mrs. Tyler?"

I said, "Tyler has been alone with the boys for several years. There is no Mrs. Tyler, and he and I would both consider it an answer to prayer if there might one day be a Mr. last-name-to-be-determined, who sees what those of us who love and care for Tyler see. Jemison men are known to be lug-heads when love comes along, so if your brother is ever interested, he'll have to make the first move."

Giles was just saying, "Very interesting," as Tyler and Christian came up to us.

Christian asked, "What's very interesting?"

Giles gave a brotherly response, "That's for us to know and you to figure out."

My mischievous self was working to contain itself. Looking straight at Tyler and Christian I said, "You boys looked like two young school girls too embarrassed to look the cute boys in the eyes. You're both pretty cute whether you know it or not. Giles, Christian, we're going to the Daisy Cafe. Nothing fancy, but I'm buying. Would you like to join us?"

Giles answered before Christian had a chance to accept or wangle out. "We'd love to."

I began herding the cats. "Let's get goin' then! Come on boys," I hollered over to Jimmy and Johnny and waved them to the door.

We lucked out at the cafe. A six top had just cleared, and the only couple waiting said they'd wait for a booth. Ethel took one look at the bunch of us and said, "August, how many boys you gonna adopt?"

I said, "You got it all wrong. I'm trying to find somebody to adopt me and none will."

Maggie came to the table with menus and said, "Yes, we have several servings of pork loin and plenty of mincemeat pie. One of us will be back to get your order shortly. I know what these four want to drink. What can I get you two new boys?"

Christian said, "Water for me."

153

Giles said, "Sweet tea for me." After Maggie was off for the drinks he asked, "Mincemeat pie? Like the stuff in the jar at the store?"

Tyler said, "Definitely not like the stuff in the store. This is homemade by Noel who runs this place, and it's from a recipe that August's mother passed on to him. I believe his ancestors brought it with them from Switzerland—or so the story goes."

"Or so the story goes," I said. "And I suppose it's one of those things you either love or hate."

Maggie was back and set the drinks down. Then she looked at me and said, "Let me guess. Pork loin and mincemeat pie. Bring the pie out first."

I just grinned at her.

"Boys?" Tyler looked at Jimmy and Johnny.

In lockstep they both replied. "Same for me."

Tyler said, "Make it four."

Christian said, "What do I know? Make it five."

Giles said "We'll keep it easy. Make it six."

"Well, that's a first for this bunch," Maggie noted and was off to the kitchen.

I saw Noel peek his head out the kitchen door looking at our table. When the pie arrived it was warm and he'd included a small dish of homemade vanilla gelato to go with it. It must be something he'd made for himself as it wasn't on the list of specials. Maggie brought the pie and Ethel set the gelato next to it as they went around the table. Ethel said, "Compliments of the chef."

Tyler smiled and said, "Please thank him for all of us."

When we were all finished with lunch—plates cleaned to a near shine, Christian said, "I can see why you come here for that Sunday special. That was excellent."

"It's good, but loud in here on Sundays," I noted. "Would y'all like to come over for coffee or tea or port or something? The Jemisons live in one half of a duplex, and I live in the other, so four of us will just be going home."

Again Giles jumped at the invitation, "We have no pressing engagements. Isn't that right brother?"

"Apparently not," Christian said with some resignation. "We'll follow you."

We all went into my apartment, where I proceeded to go to the bedroom to give Penny-girl the little bit of pork Jimmy, Johnny and I had set aside in a napkin. The boys went to their apartment to work on some homework, so they'd be done to watch TV later with their dad.

The Marvel brothers were a little taken aback when they walked in. Giles said, "When you said duplex, this wasn't exactly what sprang into mind. This is beautiful."

"Yes it is," Christian concurred.

The conversation meandered all over the place, ending where it had begun in a sense. That was Valle Crucis. Tyler told them of some of their church-search adventures and how they kept coming back to that church. He also told them about the churches in Macon, and how his Aunt Ruby and his cousin Huey both were excellent organists. He concluded saying they had decided they were going to call Valle Crucis home, at least for the time being and probably a long time, as they were in Boone to stay.

As Christian and Giles got up to leave, Christian said, "I expect we will see you there next Sunday—well, I'll be there. My brother here may or may not be out bed in time to drive out with me."

Tyler walked with them to the end of the drive. I wasn't sure if he'd come back in or just go home. I was standing in the door to wave them off. He came back up my walk.

"Well, I'll bet that's an interesting conversation in that car right now," I joked.

"Why do you think that?" Tyler asked.

"I asked Giles if Christian was moving a family here, and he made it crystal clear that Christian was looking for a good husband."

Tyler responded, "And I suppose you happened to mention someone who you thought would make a good one."

"A fellow with two nice boys came to mind at the time," I said.

Tyler smiled and said, "I may have to see just how much I meant that prayer."

Chapter Twenty-three

The next time I got a chance to have a chat with Tyler was the following Sunday afternoon. I skipped church, but he reported that the Marvel brothers were both in church again, and they all sat in the same pews as the week before.

The priest remarked afterward, "The baritone section was down one this morning. Is he all right?"

Jimmy told him I was fine and dandy, just lazy about church. I told Tyler all I can do is commend his honest and forthright telling of my absence.

I wanted to make him an offer. "Tyler, I plan to keep a wide berth as far as your personal affairs, but it did occur to me that my proximity next door might allow for a transition, of a kind, for Christian—or whoever it might be if Christian isn't the one for you—to break him in easily in getting to know the boys, and for the boys to get used to him. I could serve as a host for lunch or dinner or Saturday morning waffles and sausage—whatever. And I don't mind a bit if it is with some frequency. Just think about it, and let me know."

Tyler sat silent for a moment. "I know you really want to know if there is any spark between us like you and Miles obviously had. For me, I can say the answer to that is yes. In fact, surprisingly so. From when we walked into that pew on the wrong side of the church, I felt my heart beat through my chest for a moment. I have never experienced anything like that before. Honestly, I just wanted to stop and stare at him. And I know you told Giles about Jemison men because Christian said to me as we were leaving the church, 'I understand the Jemison men need some encouragement to get things started. I'd be glad for you to think about how I might spend some time with you and your boys.' All I could think to say was, "I'd like that."

I replied, "As you've heard me say before, the offer stands. I'm glad to be a safe place for two handsome courtin' men."

On Monday, I called Sadie. I said, "I met your new budget director at church a week ago. Seems like a top-notch fellow."

She said, "I thought you quit going to church."

I said, "I darken their door from time to time. I went with Tyler and the boys out to Valle Crucis and Christian and his brother Giles were there. We sat right in front of them, and they joined us for lunch at the Daisy Cafe."

She always gave me a hard time about the cafe. "I don't know why you don't buy that place. You'd save money as often as you eat there. But to your point, yes, Christian has been here about a month and he's wonderful!" Then she dropped to a softer tone and said, "I think he's gay."

"You have to whisper it?" I whispered back.

"My door is open and he's just outside."

I confirmed for the record, "According to his brother Giles, he would be quite content to find a good husband."

"Just as I suspected," she said.

I asked, "Have you given him some indication that such a course in his life won't mean any trouble with you?"

"No I haven't yet, but you've given me a good in, now that I know you've met. I can tell him how I worked with you, and knew you and Miles. I'll pour it on thick enough he'll know he's safe to be himself with me."

I said, "That's great. I'm rather hoping he and Tyler work out."

She acted genuinely surprised by my suggestion. "Is Tyler gay?"

"So it would seem. He's smitten with Christian."

She said, "Well, I've got to run to a meeting, but I can't wait to chat with him. If someone is going to marry into a ready-made family, one would be hard-pressed to do better than the Jemisons."

I said, "As is often the case with you, I agree completely. Take care, and we'll talk again soon."

In her usual way with me she simply said, "Ciao!" and hung up the phone—off to her next mountain to conquer.

I continued my absence from church as the Jemisons and Marvels became regulars. When the boys asked me I'd just say, "Not this week. Thanks for asking." At some point I thought I'd just drive myself out there—getting there early enough if they sat with me fine, if they didn't that was fine too. My main reason was to allow the wide berth I'd promised Tyler. And as much as I like

Noel's pork loin and mince-pie, I don't need the pie or the Sunday mayhem that prevails with the Sunday crowd.

After a month since we'd had our introductions, Tyler emailed me mid-week to take me up on my offer.

Is there any chance that me and the boys and Christian could come over to your place for dinner on Friday evening. I thought I'd make it a kind of informal after work get-together. Giles won't be there. It will be just Christian so he can get to know the boys a bit. Your friend, Tyler.

I saw the email just a couple minutes later and wrote back.

I will kill the fatted calf and get my best muumuu pressed and ready.

He pinged me right back.

We'll have to charge admission for that sight. I suspect several in town would pay to see it. 5:30 okay?

5:30 it is. If you have anything special you want for dinner, let me know. Cheers, August.

I skipped the muumuu (that I don't own) and stuck to my usual jeans and Orvis shirt. Christian arrived promptly at 5:30. I'd seen Tyler pull in shortly after 5:00, so I assumed they would be right along. They came bearing a gift. Johnny handed it to me. "Since you've been missin' Sundays we brought you a mincemeat pie."

I took it and said, "Thank you, kind sirs." My use of the term "sirs" made Jimmy snicker.

It was a pleasant evening. Everyone seemed relaxed and as though we'd gotten together in this way many times before. When it was the boys' bedtime, Tyler walked them back to the apartment and stayed with them for a time. Christian and I just made casual conversation. I shared with him some of Miles' and my life together and working backward to my Mennonite farm days. He talked about his mom going back for her Master's of Divinity and getting ordained, and how much his father loved the clock shop—though his father guessed it would die out with him unless his sister took it on. She was thinking about it.

After a few minutes Tyler came back over and said, "The boys are in bed. Jimmy was asleep by the time his head hit the pillow."

I wasn't particularly tired but I said, "This old man is going to keep Penny-girl company. She prefers I stick to my normal bedtime, or she'll be out here looking for me. You two feel free to stay as long as you like. Turn the lights out and lock the door behind you. Good night."

"Thank you, August," Tyler said, "And good night."

"Yes, thank you for a wonderful evening. Good night," Christian added.

I said, "We'll do it again, real soon."

It seemed to be a good formula for bringing Christian together with the boys. We started making it a Friday evening regular affair. Tyler and I would deliberately occupy ourselves in the kitchen when working on dinner, so that Christian and the boys would spend time alone together. After the fourth Friday when Tyler walked the boys home, I asked Christian quite directly. "Tell me what you think. Could you make a life with Tyler and his boys? You can tell me to mind my own business. I won't be offended."

He said, "I have an easy answer to that. I can't imagine my life without them."

"Well, does Tyler know that?" I asked.

He answered, "I have not said it that forthrightly."

I said, "He's crazy about you. You might want to tell it to him that forthrightly. Maybe you both got the lug-head gene for not doing what's right there in front of you to do. I know you both see it. You're both scared shitless to do anything about it seems to me."

Before he got a chance to say anything, Tyler was back from putting the boys to bed. I said, "You know where I'm going and yes, I know you appreciated the evening, blah, blah, blah. I expect the lug-head brigade better shit or git off the pot, as my Mennonite father used to say. Good night." And I closed my bedroom door behind me.

I heard the two of them burst into laughter. And then all went quiet. "Good," I thought. They don't need words to pour out what's in their hearts right this moment.

Tyler's concern over how he would tell his story in the varying accounts required had been making a logical progression. At work, people knew to this point that he was divorced and that he had full custody—his ex having left the country. That was all they really knew and all they really needed to know. By learning my story, and after our many conversations about the Jemison family and our experiences with churches, by the time he wanted to consider a relationship, all he said and needed to say was he wasn't looking for a Ruby Rose Reed. It was always the boys who concerned him most. He didn't want to tell them during the move that he and Mariah had finally divorced, but that did trigger something he hadn't anticipated. When the boys' birthdays rolled around, no card arrived from Panama. At Christmas, again there was no card. She had done this one small thing since she'd moved away, and now she'd cut herself off altogether. Tyler waited to see if either boy would say anything when the birthday card didn't arrive. Neither did. However, when the Christmas card apparently got lost between her kitchen table and the mailbox, both boys came to Tyler wanting to finally talk about their mother.

Johnny asked, "Are you divorced from Mariah?"

Johnny calling her Mariah was not lost on him. They had always referred to her simply as "our mom." Now, unsurprisingly, she had morphed into Mariah. He answered, "Yes, boys. Mariah sent me the divorce papers just as we were leaving Macon. I can't tell you much more than that because I don't know much more than that. I had a packet of papers ready to be filed with the court, but she didn't include any letter about her life or any connection she might want to keep with ours. I was surprised that the cards stopped, but without something to keep one connected, over time it becomes just easier to drift away. Do you understand that?"

Jimmy said, "I guess its kinda like the friends Johnny and I had in Macon. We don't write or call them and they don't write or call us. We've made new friends here, and they don't need us as friends there anymore either."

Tyler said, "That's about the size of it. Even relatives drift apart and, without downright determination, connections become nonexistent. Mariah likely found the cards to be a reminder that her life had not gone according to plan, and since she made the drastic step of moving out of the country, the cards were just part of the pain of what she walked away from when she left you two boys. We can't hate her for that."

Johnny piped in, "Momma Daisy taught us, the only thing hate 'ill do is eat ya from the inside out."

Tyler said, "That's exactly right. I've never hated myself or Mariah. I hope she's never hated herself or me, but I honestly have no idea if such is the case. She wanted something from me I wasn't able to give and I thought, because we were a family and had all the love of Momma and Pappy, that it would all work out. I was wrong about that. Then one day she was just gone. People don't come in perfect, even parents of near-perfect boys."

Jimmy asked, "Do you think you'll ever marry again?"

Tyler knew how he wanted to answer that and pondered the best way. He'd worked up a few answers over the years to that question, and now waited to see which one came out. "Your cousin, Vivian, had a fit when Jo Carol married Tracy."

Johnny interrupted long enough to say, "I wouldn't't've thought cousin Vivian could say anything about the way others live."

Tyler continued, "Your Aunt Ruby said as much to her. She said to her, 'Momma said, 'God gave us that girl to open our eyes.'' I knew what she meant. Jo Carol always knew who she was. Even as a small girl she was so confident in her skin that all you could do was take her for what she was. If the kids at school picked on her callin' her a 'tom-boy,' it didn't bother her a bit. She would never pick a fight, and would walk away if someone tried to start one. Of the cousins, she was the strongest, the most self assured—way stronger than me. Jo Carol opened my own eyes and forced me to reckon with something I kept locked away, afraid of what it meant."

Johnny had calculated the equation Tyler had been layin' down in their minds. "I guess you're tellin' us we ain't gonna have another momma, but we might have another daddy."

Tyler smiled at both and said, "You two are always a step ahead of me—smarter than the average bears."

It was Saturday morning. I was just up and walked through the living room—empty as I expected—but noticed outside the window, Christian's car out front. Interesting, I thought. I didn't expect to find them in my living room that morning, but neither had I envisioned a sleepover next door. I was just going into the kitchen to make coffee when there was a very soft rap on the door. It didn't resemble Tyler or the boys' usual knock. I opened the door to find Jimmy and Johnny standing there.

Johnny said, "We knocked real soft in case you was sleepin' in."

I said, "I'm up as you can see. Come on in." I closed the door and headed back to the kitchen with both boys following. "Is there something you want to ask me or tell me? Maybe something about that car parked out front?"

Johnny said, "Daddy is still asleep and Christian is asleep on the couch. I heard 'em come in real late, and we didn't want to make noise and wake them up. We were hoping we could stay over here."

I asked, "How's your dad gonna know where you are when he does get up?"

Johnny said, "I left him a note that we were comin' over here. We figured if you weren't up either, we'd just put the note in the trash."

"You boys get your good plannin' skills from your daddy," I said hoping to make them feel I was good with their early call on me. Then I said to them, "I guess if you didn't like Christian you'da rolled him off the couch and told him to go home. The fact you let him sleep must mean you think he's a pretty nice fella. Does he snore?"

They both got tickled at that. Jimmy said, "We didn't hear no snoring, but his mouth was kinda hangin' open and a little slobber was comin' out."

I smiled and said, "Well, that happens to the best of us, and the older you get the more you drool— seems like. Then, hair stops growin' where you want it and starts growin' where you don't. But you didn't answer my question as to whether you think he's a nice fella."

Johnny's answer surprised me a bit, even for these two. "Daddy lights up and looks at him the same way he does when he looks at us. I think he's gonna be our new daddy. We already know we aren't gonna get a new momma."

Jimmy added, "Our cousins, John and Thomas, got two mommas, Jo Carol and Tracy. They's adopted. Christian is real nice. I hope Daddy marries him."

I said, "So you have you told your daddy that?"

"Not yet," Jimmy said.

I asked, "You waitin' on somethin' in particular?"

It suddenly seemed to dawn on Johnny, "I don't know what we're waitin' on. Could be we're the hold-up."

I said, "Yup, it could be you are. I think you need to go back home, and each of you pick one to roll out of bed, and when they are both up say to them, 'Are you two waitin' on somethin' in particular, or are you gonna git your business done and git married?' See what they say to that."

Johnny grabbed Jimmy's hand. "Let's go Jimmy," and they were off to surprise the daddy and soon-to-be daddy next door.

An hour later, Tyler knocked on my door. I opened it and didn't say a word—just smiled at him. I didn't even invite him in. Tyler said, "Somehow those boys got the idea that Christian and I ought to be gettin' married and today's the day to git on with it. I can't imagine where they got such an idea put in to their heads. Any thoughts on that?"

"I haven't a clue," I said. "They always do their own reckonin' with the wise counsel of the Jemison heritage to guide them. Have the lug-heads come to any conclusion?"

Tyler said, "It seems the only thing left to do at the moment is plan a wedding."

I said, "I realize I might lose some good neighbors as a result of our prayin'."

He responded, "I don't think you have to worry too much about that, unless you want us out. Christian, as you know, has been stuck in that cracker-box apartment with Giles and loves our apartment. I'm pretty sure, for the time being, none of us are going anywhere."

I smiled and said, "You know how to make an old man and two boys happy. Now, go get the other lug head and those two boys and I'll make pecan waffles."

Tyler confirmed, "Sounds good to me."

The rest of the day was spent with Christian and Tyler both calling and emailing friends and relatives to tell them the news. The first call they made on speaker phone was to Christian's folks, and the first thing his mom said was, "I hope you'll consider allowing me to marry you here at the church. I'm close enough to retirement—if the bishop doesn't like it, I don't really care."

Tyler jumped in to say, "We hadn't talked about where or exactly when yet, but South Carolina would be handier for any of my family coming from Macon."

She jumped back in before Christian had a chance to derail such a notion, "Well, there you go, son. Sounds like we're going to have a wedding in Columbia."

Christian joked, "It sounds like the take-charge priest and city manager made that decision without the clock master and budget manager having any input. Dad, sounds like this might be a sign of things to come."

Christian's dad said, "It's the way of our world, but not one I'd trade off, would you?"

He responded, "No, I think we both have done pretty well finding love."

His mom said, "Tyler, you see how they butter us up?"

Tyler laughed, "A little butter and a little sugar goes a long way with me."

Turning to a timeframe Christian said, "We're thinking about something around the 4th of July. There's a lot of Jemison family history I need to tell you about as to why that is, but I'll put that in an email to you. It won't be a flag-flying wedding. Let's leave it at that for the moment. Will that work for you, Mom?"

"Certainly, Son."

Tyler said, "We'll let everyone know that's our tentative plan then. Christian tells me your church has a nice pipe organ. My cousin, Huey, is a concert organist. If he's free, would it be okay if he played and worked with you planning the service? He's our official family ceremony planner."

His dad said, "Your cousin is Huey Jemison? He played here at the cathedral last year. Outstanding! Really outstanding! We were so taken with his spirit and humility, which the latter is sometimes hard to find in people of his level of talent."

His mom added, "You could see he felt it was all gift, and he was just giving back his portion."

"That is very aptly put, Mrs. Marvel," Tyler said.

She said, "Mother, Mom or Hey-you will do. You don't need to call me Mrs. Marvel. Certainly, you tell Huey it would be a great honor to have him here and to have his help planning the service."

"That's wonderful," Tyler said.

Christian said, "Thanks, Mom and Dad. We'd better get on letting everyone else know. Take care."

And the good priest offered her benediction. "Bless and keep you both. Bye for now."

Both spent that afternoon mostly sending emails, with a few calls where it seemed more fitting. Tyler called Ira and Ruby, and then Claudine. When he told Ira and Ruby, he said he also wanted to run something by Ira. "Uncle Ira, do you think it would be disrespectful to my daddy, you or anyone in the family—living or dead—if I was to be married on the 4th?"

Tyler didn't expect an instant knee-jerk answer one way or the other. He expected Ira to ponder his answer, which Ira did. It was his way to consider carefully whatever was put to him. When he'd run things through in his own mind he answered, "Tyler, I suspect you're thinkin' about this the same way my mind is right now. That day changed this family forever. I have to ask, will it always be a day for mourning, or can some light come into it after all these years? It means the world to me that you'd put the question to me, since I'm the only one left of that generation—and the generation before it that carried the loss the hardest is gone as well. I'll speak for the dead and the living, and if any of the living have a problem with it, they'll have to take it up with me. You tell all your cousins, "Uncle Ira says there's only one date for this weddin' to take place and that's the 4th of July.""

Most of the cousins he would blanket with an email once the necessary calls were made. Some might have already heard by then, but he couldn't see how that would matter. He went back and forth on calling Dewayne and Jo Carol and decided to give them both a call. He wasn't exactly sure how Dewayne would react, but chanced it. His reaction took him by surprise—more like shock.

Dewayne said, "When I first started working with Daddy laying rock he once said to me, 'That boy Tyler's gonna have to face up to the truth of what he is one of these days. I love him, but he's only foolin' himself. But what foolin' he did, brought forth two wonderful boys that were pure gifts from God.' Daddy would be glad to hear you're gettin' hitched proper this time."

With that reaction, Tyler had the courage to ask what he'd hoped he could, and the reason he wanted to call rather than email Dewayne in the first place. "Dewayne, I'd like you to consider being my best man. If you're not comfortable with it, I don't want you to feel in any way obligated."

Dewayne chuckled a bit. "It occurs to me, since I'm the only one of your kin that is nearly as big as Momma Daisy, that it's only fittin' that I stand up there for her and Pappy. I think that would make them both happy, and I am more than happy to do it."

Between the announcement and the wedding, Penny-girl had finally come to her end, joining her sister Bonnie, the goldens and Miles in the backyard cemetery. Tyler, Christian and the boys came over to be there when I'd laid her in the ground. The boys were the only other people beside Miles and me she ever took to. I thought, if they wanted to be there when I buried her they should be. And so they all came over.

I took off her collar and laid it and her leash next to her, as I had done with the others before her. I covered her up and said, "All these interred here were given good Christian burials. No big fuss, but always a prayer of gratitude for what they brought into my life. After Penny-girl's stone gets here and is placed on her grave, there'll be only one more stone needed. It might be up to one of you to place it when the time comes."

Huey was going to be able to play for the wedding. He and Christian's mom presented Tyler and Christian with their plan for a very nice service and reception. Standing with Tyler would be Dewayne, Johnny, Jimmy and Billy. Standing with Christian would be Giles, his dad and his sister, who was mid-way in age between Christian and Giles.

Someone from the church had written to the bishop when they heard the rector was going to be marrying her own son to another man. She saw a letter from the bishop's office and didn't really care what it said inside one way or the other. She stuck it unopened into her desk drawer and proceeded as though she didn't have a worry in the world. It was so close to the date now, she thought whoever it was in the parish couldn't do much about it at that point. She also had more than a fair idea of who sent the letter, and had hoped something would either finally bring him around or push him far enough to leave once and for all. She had grown tired of his constant refrain against anything he deemed unorthodox—which she knew went all the way back to the abandonment of the sacrosanct 1928 Prayer Book, followed by initiating the Eucharist every Sunday to, of course, women being ordained and then a gay bishop in New Hampshire. And so it continued. She knew the vestry not only supported her, but would attend in full force as a sign of solidarity for this first "gay wedding" in the parish.

Sadie—my old boss and Christian's current boss—rode down with me to Columbia. We'd both been invited to join the families for the rehearsal dinner and both gratefully accepted. On the drive down, she caught me up on all the university drama which was never in short supply. That conversation pretty well filled about two of the three-hour drive. Then she said it was the first time she'd ever gone to a wedding on the 4th of July—couldn't even recall any wedding on that day. She guessed they wanted lots of fireworks at their reception. I said, "Well, I think you're in for a surprise there." And I proceeded to lay out all the history from July 4, 1971, to Momma Daisy's night-time burial in the chicken run, to her annual recitation of the twenty-second Psalm, and all her well-known chosen words she put forth for each of these which now were a rich part of the family legacy. I was even able to tell her of Ira's confirmation of the date and how he laid out his thoughts to Tyler.

By the time I was through, I could hardly drive for the tears in my eyes, and this stalwart CFO was sobbing and blowing her nose like we'd both known and loved Horatio Spafford Jemison—and that his life had been cut out of ours as it had been from theirs. Such was the impact the Jemisons had on my life and was now having on hers.

With just a three-hour or so drive from Macon, almost all Tyler's cousins came up for the wedding. They'd been prompted to do so by Dewayne and equally encouraged to do so by Ira, Ruby and Claudine. It had been months since Ruby and Ira had heard from Vivian. Billy was the youngest boy of that generation, but he had two younger female cousins, Maya Jean and Margaret Mary, grandchildren of Claudine. Claudine encouraged her daughter, Martha Marie, to have the girls spend time with Billy so that he would feel connected to that generation of Jemisons, particularly since he hadn't seen any of his brothers or sisters since he went to live with Ira and Ruby. Except for the Washington mess, all the living relatives from Macon made the trip to Columbia.

The ushers had been instructed to seat us with the family. Rather than split from one side to the other we both sat on the Jemison side since, with the local church family, the pews were loaded in the Marvel favor already. I hadn't been in a Church of God now for decades, but I smiled as I heard Huey working in some up-beat improvisations of old Church of God hymns. I thought Momma Daisy and Pappy would be smiling to hear Huey-boy workin' those songs into the Episcopalians. I didn't figure we'd hear *Here Comes the Bride* and we didn't. It was more like a Sunday morning festival procession than the typical wedding. Huey ended the prelude music and the church bells were rung for at least two full minutes. I thought, "About time." The only place I ever hear church bells rung "proper" is on my trips to Switzerland. They'd consider a couple of minutes just getting warmed up, but it was sure better than the pitiful clap or two that most churches that have a bell ever muster in this country. And most churches have no bell. As the bells were ending, Huey blew everyone to their feet with the en chamade stop—the festival reed pipes that projected straight out into the sanctuary. It was his own arrangement of Vaughn Williams' *Salve Festa Dies—Hail Thee Festival Day*. Down the aisle came James and Claudine's four grandchildren, who knew the Episcopal drill from serving in the church in Macon— thurifer first —smoke billowing, with two acolytes following, then the crucifier, the wedding party—dressed in white albs and each wearing large, very striking coral handcrafted necklaces that Ruby had made for Ira's hand-carved wooden ankh-style crosses—then Jo Carol carrying the Gospel book, followed by Tyler and Christian, both walking side by side in very handsome matching beige and gold sherwanis, and finally Christian's mother in her white alb and white and gold brocade chasuble. When all were in their places, Huey finished the piece with the en chamade pipes and antiphonal organ, holding the last grand chord for nearly a full minute. My companion leaned over to me and said, "Wow!"

When the priest turned around to begin, she saw an uninvited guest. Halfway back on the Jemison side, was a man with a purple shirt and white collar under his dark jacket. It was her bishop. She was trying to decide if she should skip the line about anyone speaking now or forever holding their peace. But she was always quick on her feet and had contemplated what she would say if the troublemaker crashed the service and spoke up at that time. She was glad the troublemaker was not there and proceeded with the question, trying not to let it be known she'd seen the bishop in the crowd. Her bishop wasn't shy. Would he try to put a stop to this? ...No reaction from him or anyone else!

It all went off a without hitch. For the recessional, Huey played his organ transcription of the Finale from Saint-Saens' Symphony No. 3. It was as beautiful a wedding as I'd ever attended which, one must grant, isn't saying much coming from me, but my companion agreed. I said to Sadie, "All these years I've known you I've only ever seen you cry twice, and that's been in the last two days. You must be getting soft in your old age."

She said, "It's not my age. It's those Jemisons."

As we neared the door, you could hear the carillon pealing in great splendor the celebration of this day redeemed in love for all the Jemisons living and dead. For me, no funky mood anywhere in sight.

Not surprisingly, the bishop cornered Christian's mother afterwards. "I got one letter from a member of this parish who wrote to tell me he knew I agreed with him that such a thing can't take place in this church. I also got a letter signed by every member of the vestry who said such a thing can and should take place. Both tried to be persuasive. You didn't call me as I asked in my letter for you to do."

She said, "I might have misplaced that on my desk before opening it."

"How convenient," he replied and continued, "I was going to call you when I got a call from a friend of the Jemisons, a Mr. August Kibler. If you know who he is, I'd like you to point him out to me. He asked me to be patient as he laid out a story of a man and two boys, which he proceeded to do for the next half hour or so. It was during that call that I made the connection with Huey being a part of the same family who I, of course, met when he played at the cathedral. Mr. Kibler concluded by saying to me, 'Bishop, I've lived my life from the working assumption that with my doubts I might be wrong, but that is a far better way than being certainly wrong. To inflict hurt on the Jemison family would be certainly wrong.' I came here to see this man and his two boys, and the old man who took 'a chisel to my bound conscience and opened up enough of a crack for a little of Momma Daisy's light to come in,' as Mr. Kibler would put it.

She said, "The old man you are looking for isn't much older than you, but you'll find him right over there."

I saw the bishop headed my way who, of course, had no idea of my history with bishops, but with whom I'd now forged yet another history. He approached with his hand out, "So you'd be August Kibler."

I shook his hand, "And you'd be the bishop."

Chapter Twenty-four

The new family needed to work out their new arrangement. It was assumed Tyler would remain Daddy as one would expect. Tyler didn't want the boys to call Christian by his first name, but didn't want to confuse things either. A family meeting was held. The boys decided they wanted to call Christian, Papi. When the boys told me the name they'd settled on, I said to them, "Oh, puppy! That's so nice. He is cute like a puppy."

They replied in unison, "Not puppy—Papi!"

I smiled at them and said, "I was just teasin' ya."

The remainder of the summer saw legal affairs attended to as a priority—theirs and mine. They would complete name changes and full adoption of the boys. They were now legally Johnny Ira Marvel-Jemison and Jimmy Martin Marvel-Jemison. Tyler also registered their names with the school as such, though he thought they might turn in the assignments as simply Jemisons. He wasn't going to tell them what to do on that, one way or the other. He thought they might feel it was easier to fit in without a hyphenated last name. Such a last name wasn't a foreign concept to them. They were used to their twin cousins, John and Thomas, whose last name since they were adopted as toddlers by Jo Carol and Tracy was Jemison-Somerset. As it turned out, both boys thought the name Marvel stood out from most, and they were always the only Jemisons in school so they were eager to put the two together. They began introducing themselves using both names. In the fall, they would turn in their homework the same way.

The legal matters I was going to attend to were substantial. When I designed the duplex, I drew it with the idea that it could be easily modified from its dual 2/2 layout into 3/3 and 1/1 apartments. I wasn't exactly sure why I didn't do this sooner, but with Christian now next door I knew I needed to "git er done." I arranged for a contractor to come over when I knew they'd all be out of the apartment, explained the door structure we had built into the walls between the two apartments, and how I wanted to close off the portions on my side. He could start in about three weeks and said it would take less than a week. If he'd said any longer, I'd have gone shopping for a different contractor. As he laid things out, it sounded exactly right to me as far as price and hours to do the work. I never did put in separate electrical or water meters, so it really didn't matter about any of that.

We shook on the deal, and I invited the Marvel-Jemison family over for Saturday pecan waffles. Our Saturday breakfasts were less frequent with their schedules, but we still managed to get together at least once a month. Over the years, we were in a certain rhythm with the tasks, and I had begun to turn my role over to Christian once I had his pair of hands to add to the mix. The boys always set the table, which included a glass of water for the men and their orange La Croix for themselves. They would also make us a fresh pot of coffee. Tyler would put the oven on low and stick the plates in to warm. He'd melt the butter in one skillet with the pecans— which were the base for our waffle toppings—and he would cook the Purnell all natural sausage patties, which I had to always order directly from Purnell. I would be the waffle maker. I always made a big batch of the dry ingredients and just measured out what we needed for the day, to which I would add the coconut oil, eggs, cream and water, as needed, to get to the right consistency. Today I was turning the waffle production fully over to Christian.

I leaned back against the counter and started my verbal last will and testament. "I have changed my will and related matters numerous times over the years. My executor has been my lawyer in town each time. I do want to change that if you are amenable. I'd like the two of you to be listed when I next update it."

Both Christian and Tyler said they'd be glad to handle things for me. I continued, "I have a niece who I never see, but with whom I have kept regular correspondence for years. She has long been our designated general power of attorney as well as health directive power of attorney. I'll probably leave that as is, but Tyler, I would like to put you down as alternate for both documents. Is that all right?"

Tyler said, "Of course, if that's what you want, I'll certainly do it."

I said, "It would give me peace of mind. Then there is the estate itself. I'm not a wealthy man, but with my state retirement it should see me out. I have beneficiaries and POD's on the few accounts I have. As executors, I will give you a list of those accounts. I'm trying to avoid the little bit I have going through probate. After breakfast, I have something to show you and will cover the rest then."

I'm sure they were wondering what I was going to show them, but they didn't press me. When we were done eating, we did our usual dance of the kitchen cleanup. Miles and I never used a dishwasher. We preferred to wash by hand. I had a twenty-four inch cabinet by the sink if anyone ever wanted to put one in. Of course, the same was true next door. The only renters who ever asked about putting one in were a couple of the transient faculty. What a single person needed a dishwasher for was beyond me, so I always refused. When Tyler and the boys moved in I did offer, and Tyler said he was fine without one.

With the cleanup done I said, "Follow me." I took them into Miles' bedroom and proceeded to lay out the plan. "When we built this, I designed this room to be able to reconfigure the apartments from two beds and two baths, to your side becoming a three bed and three bath—so this side could be a guest house or vacation rental or just rented out as a one bedroom. Don't ask me why I waited to do this. Somehow before Christian came along I'd rather forgotten about it. Who goes where, is your doing. My thought was, this would be Daddy and Papi's room and each of the boys would have their own room across the way. I've already got someone lined up to do the work, which will only take a few days. How's that sound?"

Tyler said, "I've learned not to ask you if you're sure you want to do something as you don't offer if you're not ready to do it. That being said, I think it sounds great! And as would be right and should have happened long ago, we can easily afford to pay what the place is actually worth and not the measly four hundred you've taken all these years. I'm sure half of that at least goes for the electric. How does two-k a month sound?"

I replied, "It doesn't sound good to me at all. You'll recall, this conversation started with me talking about my will and not wanting an estate to have to probate. Here is what I want from you. I'd like to proceed immediately with passing title to the entire property over to you two. In exchange, I'd like to live here rent free for as long as I can live on my own and am of sound mind. You and my niece can decide when a care facility needs to take me off your hands. I do not expect you to take such care on for yourselves."

After the kitchen cleanup, the boys had wandered off into the backyard, and we were standing just outside the bedroom. Christian said, "I think I need to sit down."

We moved back to the kitchen table to sit where we could see the boys. Tyler hadn't made a sound.

I asked, "Well, Tyler, what say ye?"

He just sat there glassy-eyed and more dazed than I'd ever seen him.

Christian said, "I don't think he can talk right now."

"I'm gathering that," I acknowledged. "Let's just sit quiet for a minute."

By the time Tyler was ready to say something, I don't think he wanted to look me in the eye. He got up and stood behind me with a hand on each of my shoulders. From there he could see his boys out on the swing. He started in. "I could jot down a long list of facts of my life that, if anybody picked it up, would just as quickly put it back down as nothing to see here. But there are some things that are hard to put on a list, because they aren't anything earned or sought. Some of that has carried with it great grief, like that horrible death on the 4th of July—then great joy when all those years later, that day would be redeemed in a way that would again change my life. That's a rambling way of saying, what may pass for some as an ordinary life has been anything but. My life has been extraordinary and that is thanks to the Jemisons before me, the boys that follow me, a husband who loves me, and a kindly man we happened in on one breakfast at the Daisy Cafe who became father, grandfather and most of all friend."

Christian came to put his arm around Tyler. I put my head back to look up at both of them and with a smile said, "I'll take that as a 'yes' to me living here rent free."

Maybe it was the liberation of living rent free. All of a sudden, I found myself wanting to write down Bible stories that challenged those I'd been taught; the ones that I had expressed to Tyler had been problems for me with much of Sunday school. It wasn't going to be a curriculum by any stretch. At best, it would be an expression of my own tiny systematic theology no bishop would likely find compelling. Maybe the men next door would. I didn't set out with any plan or any thought to which stories I would tell. I just started writing one day and that led to another and another and another. I started with the shepherds in the New Testament, but when it was all said and done I had just as many or more from the Old Testament. Some, it must be said, were characters plucked out of obscurity even for me and my familiarity with the Old Testament. I'm not sure how they came into the works. I tried to point out some of the conveniently overlooked verses that were a direct counter narrative to both the simple Bible story as commonly told and the subversive texts against empire—including the kings of Israel which were there and largely left out of the lectionary. Some were stories of more fantasy than chapter-and-verse adherence, but were plausible wanderings of the spirit moving through the text. Well, perhaps only plausible to me. It's for others to decide for themselves.

In the course of about three weeks I had them done. They included the two black characters in the New Testament, Simon of Cyrene and the Ethiopian Eunuch, which was not by design but happened as naturally as all the others. I printed it up and put it in a three-ring binder with a cover sheet that read simply, "Stories for Tyler, by August Kibler." I gave it to him saying, "You've heard me talk about churches enough. This might be the best way of passing along where I've ended up. You may keep it or toss it or share it as you see fit."

I was determined to never ask about them. It wasn't an exercise in vanity as best I could determine. They came from someplace inside that was mysterious and inexplicable. Whether I just needed to put it all down for my sake or someone else's I couldn't say. In time, I knew that Tyler was sharing them with the boys—I should say young men. They began to make reference to some of the characters. Christian asked if he could share a copy with his mom. I said sure and sent him a pdf copy.

A few weeks later Tyler said, "It would have been real interesting if you and Momma could have talked about these stories. I'll bet she might have come up with some others of her own to add to it. They do come alive as you read them."

No longer a single-parent household, the Marvel-Jemison family was able to juggle more with the boys than when Tyler was alone with only me to help out here and there. They got involved in soccer and piano and contemporary-dance lessons, and the boys started serving as acolytes at Valle Crucis. Both Christian and Tyler were in the regular rotation of eucharistic ministers and lay readers. Both followed my advice to this point—avoid getting on the vestry or ever getting snared into being church treasurer. They both would have been great assets in those roles, but it is a slippery slope I went sliding down and thought it only fair to warn them. I was just as determined not to chastise them if they didn't take my advice, though with the boys and work neither was looking for martyrdom in church administration.

Johnny and Jimmy had been instructed by their dads to be sure I was given a schedule of their games and recitals. Whenever I got the schedules, I told them I'd be sure to get a copy down to Ethel, Maggie and Noel so they'd know to be cheering them on if not actually present. Ethel or Maggie did on occasion show up to something the boys were in. All my cafe friends were most amused that I would be attending the boys' soccer games and recitals. I didn't always make every game, but many, and given the lesser frequency of recitals found it easy enough to make all those. When I could, I'd persuade Layla and Amelia to join me for old times' sake, and we would always end up at one or the other's home drinking wine afterwards.

I also continued our summer ritual of Operation Jemison Boys as their busier schedules would allow. We got off to a late start the summer following the big wedding. With Penny-girl gone, I decided to take the long-planned trip that Miles and I were going to take and never got the chance. So the first week of May, I headed to Zurich for the eight-week stay, with a week in Bavaria, two weeks in France and the rest of the time in Switzerland. The first part of the trip I rented a car, and for the remainder I got my first class Swiss pass and went merrily from place to place. I managed to get to a few church services when the bells rang, as Miles and I had done so many times, while successfully avoiding funerals this trip. I thought the fact that I failed to crash one would be a disappointment to him, but not too tragic. It was the first trip I'd ever sent so many postcards. I never bothered much in the past. Now, it's so easy to email photos for free, postcards seem obsolete. But I thought so am I, so I sent postcards to everyone from the Marvel-Jemisons to the cafe to John Cross to the few old college connections I still had—hell, I even sent one to the bishop.

From the start, I approached the trip with the notion that this would be my last trip to Europe. Partly, because I've been there more than most would ever have the chance to be, and I thought I should tell myself, "enough is enough." Yes, the grass *is* greener there, but North Carolina is beautiful, too. It was also because I had observed people too old to travel well or safely still hanging on to their travel routine, and I would look at them and think, "enough *is* enough." I didn't want to be looked on with pity the way I looked on them. "Do unto others" as the saying goes. I wouldn't inflict my frailty on others if I could help it. I relented a little bit in my mind as I thought about how I could plan a trip for my family next door. It would, of course, have to be in the summer when the boys are out of school and thus in high season, but I also thought what a fifth wheel I would be to the works and dismissed it as quickly as it came. I could share with them all my previously printed travel plans I'd done for each trip, and they could use, or not use, whatever of that they wanted should they ever choose to go where Miles and/or I had been.

Because of my Swiss roots, it's easy enough to recognize in the various villages, or observe on the trains and boats, people who remind me of my childhood—relatives, neighbors, people from church. I'd grown quite accustomed to this degree of familiarity in my surroundings. Of course, I never stopped people to say how they reminded me of someone. I'm not that loony—yet. While I was staying in a chalet on Thunersee, I boarded the steamer for a ride over to Interlaken. I was out on the open deck enjoying the clear sunny day, the deep blue-green of the lake and the still-snowy peaks of the alps. Then, I also saw a woman roughly my age, and I looked at who she was with. She had to be my old neighbor. I'd only met her husband once or twice and hadn't seen her in many years—not since my mother's funeral, in fact. I thought, perhaps if I moved closer to them she might see me and have the same revelation. I moseyed my way towards the rail of the steamer half turning towards them and glanced their direction. Then I heard it, "August?" She said it loud enough to be heard, but not so much as to be discernible as to whom she was directing the question. I said, "I thought that had to be you, but what are the odds?"

She jumped up and hugged me. "I can't believe it!"

I said, "Your dad's family and my mom's came from these villages right here on Lake Thun. Seems fitting we run into each other here." I knew she would know this as I had some years earlier shared with them the ancestry work I had done. Technically, we were distant relatives. My great-grandfather and her great-grandmother were brother and sister. As kids we didn't really know or appreciate that connection. We were just neighbor kids who rode the bus to school together, would sled and skate together in the winter, and would take our big steers to the county fair together. Our families were close friends, and we always ushered in the new year—one year at our house, the next at theirs. Her dad gave me my first dog, and I had great admiration for that peaceable man—also Mennonite. Neither they nor I had pressing plans that day so I accepted their invitation to tag along. We spent the next two days together before they went one direction in their travels and I went another.

It is remarkable how easy it is to connect with people when one isn't concerned about an agenda or asserting one's need to be right. I suppose the best word for that is humility. It offers the chance to take people as they come without dissection to see if we approve. It might be, if I and my old neighbor spent a lot of time together, we would come to irreconcilable differences—but when you look for joy and gratitude, those differences are not likely to be found. We had found ourselves in our foremothers' and forefathers' native land and celebrated all our common bond had to offer. As Tyler had explained to his boys about people growing distant, I certainly have gone there myself as I think about these, my childhood neighbors. Nothing really had separated us but miles and years, and the family that would be theirs and the family that would be mine.

That can't be said about some friends and family. I've felt estranged from many over time—just a result of politics, religion, and even family drama that makes for strained relations. Certitude, pride, intolerance, hate and fear fuel so much division. We see it plainly enough at the macro-level of nationalism (another ism) and forget the seeds sown and nourished in the micro-level of our own hearts. My trips to the beauty of Switzerland always made me reflect on a heart of *what can be* rather than the tyrannical grip that poisons so much of our world of *what must be*.

In June, while I was still in Switzerland, the Marvel-Jemison family made their first trip back to Macon for a week's stay. Tyler wasn't sure how it would feel to go back after so much time had passed, or how it would look in reality compared to how he had filed it away in his mind. When word was out that they were coming, they had multiple offers to bunk in at one or the other's homes, but they decided to stay in a hotel which they thought would give them a little more freedom to come and go to different peoples' homes as the days passed.

Ira and Ruby's daughter, Joan, had bought Momma Daisy and Pappy's home when Tyler moved to Boone. Tyler had been glad that someone in the family wanted it. It seemed a little strange to see the name "Black" on the mailbox, but of course, that was the family living there now. He knew from Uncle Ira that the chicken run was still intact. Joan and her husband, Frederick, kept the coop full and had added a number of more exotic breeds over the years. "Them chickens still shittin' where they need to be shittin'," Tyler told Christian. Claudine continued to take the cleanings out of the coop for compost for her garden, which was now a full-family affair with her kids and grandkids all helping her.

While they were there, Dewayne organized a Jemison barbecue and potluck get-together for Sunday afternoon. Vivian remained distant from Ira and Ruby and seemed to have forgotten Billy, but Dewayne inquired as to inviting the Washington mess anyway. Ruby suggested the invitation might just as well get lost between the kitchen table and the mail box. Tyler drove his family by the place out on Johnson Road.

He drove by as slow as he could without stopping altogether. "Lord, have mercy. Look at that place. It's even worse than I remember."

It was bad. Any old toilet, appliance, chair, hot water heater, old car, truck was just so much trash piled up in front of and on both sides of that doublewide, which had pieces of blue tarp for roofing and mold all over the outside.

Christian said, "Are we sure they're alive in there? When were they last seen?"

Tyler responded, "Does make you wonder. I can't imagine living like that."

Guessing Jimmy was working out the comparison to their home he said, "Mr. August would say, 'Now that's a real show place!'"

When they got back to town they stopped at Ira and Ruby's. They were both out in their respective workshops. Ira had the door of the shop open, and he saw them drive in. He offered a tour of the shops for Christian's sake, and then they all went into the house. Billy had been in the shop with Ruby. He, Johnny and Jimmy went off to find their own adventure.

Tyler said, "I'm reluctant to pick at the old wound, but we drove by the Washingtons. Do you hear anything from them?"

Ira said, "We hear about them plenty. We hear from them never. If I see Joab with any of the kids in a store, he turns around and heads the other way. Can't say I mind altogether. If we see Vivian, she speaks enough to acknowledge our existence and that's about the extent of that. Last time we saw her Billy was with us. She looked down at him at one point and never said a word to him."

Ruby added, "So as you can see, all prayers unanswered as far as that bunch goes. Their oldest boy has already been sent to juvie for his first home away from home. He was there for nearly a year. We only know this from the Macon grapevine. I'm sure it's only the start of more state-funded accommodations to come."

Ira said, "On a more pleasant note, Jo Carol has been thinking about going to seminary. The Methodists won't support her so, she met with the rector at Claudine's church who got her in touch with the bishop. We shall see how that goes. She'll likely need to first move to a different diocese to get accepted into seminary, which would mean them moving away from here, of course. I'd hate to see them go, but as you well know, sometimes it is the right thing to do if for the right reasons. We'll just have to wait and see what Momma and Pappy are workin' out for them as they did for you."

Ruby noted her displeasure with her own denomination. "We seem to be splitting right down the middle. It could be all the Jemisons are going to be over at Claudine's church before it's over."

Both were already aware that Tyler and the boys had joined Christian and been confirmed in the Episcopal church.

Unbeknownst to the rest of the family, while they were in Macon, Tyler arranged to meet with the city. He wanted to see about the possibility of having a large open-air pavilion built at Central City Park in memory of Momma Daisy, Pappy, Uncle James and his daddy. Tyler had taken a set of plans along that the Boone city architect had done gratis for him. It would, of course, be timber frame. He was pretty sure Ira and Ruby would think it too big a project for them at this stage, but he told the city they should be given right of first refusal. Dewayne's crew would be asked to do all the stone work it required. Given the reputations of the Jemisons, the city had no problem with Tyler's plan. They moved forward with the project. The Marvel-Jemisons would, for sure, go back down to Macon for the dedication, which Tyler requested be on the following July 4th.

When next summer rolled around, the plans were finalized for the dedication. I was invited to join them. Christian said he would rent a van and hoped I'd come with them. If he hadn't worked out how we were going to get there I would have passed, but since he had I said I'd go.

Tyler told me I had to go saying, "After all you paid for it."

I said, "How do you figure that?"

Tyler said, "Years of uncollected rent."

I wanted assurance of one thing. "I'll go, but you have to promise me that such credit as you seem to want to give isn't offered to the crowd in Macon. I'll go as a friend to the Jemisons and not as a benefactor to the cause, or I don't go at all."

"I will honor that," Tyler replied.

Dewayne and his crew were going to cook-up the barbecue as was now the long-standing tradition, and he still was excited to organize these big cookouts. He was in his element. On the ride down, we all suspected Vivian and Joab would show for this, since free food was involved with minimal family interaction required. It started at 11:00, with the Mayor presiding over the dedication and the community meal to follow. There was a good crowd, and Huey had arranged to bring in a choir and ensemble to provide music for the event. Speeches were kept to a minimum. Tyler would speak for the family.

"When the boys and I left Macon six years ago, the community generously gave us a send-off in this same park, and with it a check to help us towards a start to our new life in North Carolina. Now, we are here to give back to the community this pavilion—dedicated to my father who was killed on this day soon after I was born, to the grandparents who raised me, and to my uncle whose descendants here today ensure the Jemison legacy continues. And my only living uncle doesn't know this, but the plaque also reads, "And in thanksgiving for Ira Lewis Jemison."

I was seated next to Ira who started to cry. I heard him mutter, "That boy." Then he whispered to Ruby, "Did you know he was gonna do that?" She just shook her head "no" and was crying herself.

Tyler went back to his seat and the choir stood; the music ensemble poised to begin. Huey directed them in what was the final item on the program. The first quiet strains of two french horns and a single cello played the introduction. And the choir started....

When peace like a river, attendeth my way. When sorrows like sea billows roll. Whatever my lot, thou hast taught me to say. It is well, it is well, with my soul...

With that, the only thing left to do for this old man was join Ira and Ruby and let the tears run down my cheeks.

Notes from Tyler

The routines of life were carrying us all along. Two years had passed since the dedication of the pavilion. The boys, now young men. Johnny would graduate high school this year. Jimmy thought if he put his mind to it, he could graduate a year ahead of time. We all knew if he put his mind to it, it would be done. August announced his intention of taking his first cruise, to escape some of the winter for a change. Well in advance, he booked a 15-day itinerary for February the following year and waited for the trip as a matter of course. In the meantime, he would go on with his life as a Daisy Cafe regular and tag-along friend of his "landlords," as he referred to me and Christian.

When winter rolled around and the trip grew closer, he looked forward to it more than he had expected. It seemed to him it had been colder than usual. Some warm sunshine would be a welcome change.

Each day of the trip, he would drop us a quick email. Less than a week into the trip, people started getting sick on board. Before any really knew what had hit them, they found themselves in quarantine on board the ship. August was okay—at least he thought he was—but he knew the "Marvel-Jemisons" would be concerned. Then nine days into the trip, I got my last email from him.

Dear friend, I'm sure you've probably heard by now that our ship is unable to dock anywhere at the moment. Quite a few people have the virus. I was diagnosed with it late yesterday afternoon. You know I'm pretty healthy and may be just fine, but I'm also not so arrogant or naive as to think I couldn't be one of the statistics. A lot seems unknown at the moment as to the best way to handle it in such a confined place as this—maybe any place. I don't want you to worry, but know that whatever comes, as you told me once of your own life, mine has been extraordinary! You know what to do with me if I come back home as a bag of ashes.

I love you all. August

Elegy to Mr. August
by Tyler Ethen Marvel-Jemison
for Johnny & Jimmy

Across the room the unfamiliar man
in the unfamiliar place
waved a father and two small boys
to join him in the busy cafe.
Our journey together begun.
Our life here made rich from grace upon grace.

You gave us many gifts that have no price.
You reminded us that joy and gratitude
can come from our symbols of grief—
a dog tag, a rosary, an old rocking chair.
What is our symbol for your life to be?

Perhaps it is every wooden peg of the home
you made here all those years—
first with Miles and then for and with us.
Perhaps it would be the man we met in church,
we see every day now, whose presence in our
lives you confirmed as good.
Perhaps most of all it will be in the garden
as the daisies bloom
for these remind us of your first days in our lives.

We laid your stone today
over the ashes that came to us by courier.
The few invited came.
Sadie, Madi, Layla, Amelia, Ethel, Maggie, Noel, John
Jimmy, Johnny, Christian, Tyler.
We saw to it you got the burial
you requested and nothing more.
The backyard cemetery now complete.
On the stone, the instructions as laid out by you.

August Henri Kibler
1956-2020

Made in the USA
Coppell, TX
20 July 2020